G

(What if the gravitational constant... isn't?)

a novel by
Paul Holland

Published by SWG Marketing LLC, Little Falls, NJ

PAPERBACK ISBN 978-0-9722059-3-1

Dedication:

To everyone who ever looked up at the night sky and said, wow…

A brief introduction:

The term "G" refers to the acceleration exerted by Earth's gravity equal to 32ft/sec^2.

For example you will hear things like; the shuttle astronaut was subjected to 3 G's during launch, or three times the force exerted by Earth's gravity.

It is a constant value – it never changes.

But science hates the word never. The greatest enemy in the advance of knowledge is thinking that we know something.

Answers require no thought, only acceptance.

Questions on the other hand make us think, ponder, worry, hope, extrapolate, interpret and question some more...

Answers are specific to a person, place, thing or time. They have a beginning and an end.

Questions are infinite and eternal.

So I began by asking how come we are so darn certain that the acceleration of gravity has always been the same when we really don't understand what gravity is or how it works?

And if it wasn't always the same – does that mean it can be changed?

Here's the can of worms that question opened.

Foreword

"…consider the death of a star, such as our sun.

Accepted science tells us the sun will go nova and become a red giant. It will expand such that it will engulf the innermost planets, including earth, then shrink back to become a white dwarf before dying out completely. It will then simply be a massive burned out core floating in the ever expanding universe.

But if gravity is strictly a function of mass and a star loses mass over the course of its life - how can a star exert more gravity at end of life? For example:

•The Sun has an estimated life span of 9 Billion years.

•The mass of the Sun is estimated to be 1.9882×10^{23} metric tons.

•The Sun emits an estimated 3.8×10^{26} joules / second.

•Using Einstein's formula, $E=Mc^2$ this would infer that the mass of the Sun is being lost at a rate of approximately 15 Billion metric tons per hour.

From this we can infer our Sun has lost 6×10^{20} metric tons of mass since its inception. At end of life, the Sun's rate of energy emission is anticipated to increase by approximately 10% implying that at least another 6×10^{20} metric tons will be lost. Granted that this represents only about 1/10 of a percent of the star's total mass but one wonders at what point it might be enough to upset the delicate balance of forces that maintain the planetary orbits. Prior to the demise of the star wouldn't its celestial captives depart unless there exists something else in play. Yet collapsing stars draw matter in despite the fact they are losing mass.

In 1850, the physicist Hermann von Helmholtz proposed that the source of the sun's emitted energy could be gravitation. We know of course that to be insufficient and that the source is nuclear, however it is the intense gravitational force of the Sun that confines the reaction.

It is logical that the star would become a red giant toward end of life as the it's loss of mass over time would reduce the star's ability to confine the reaction gravitationally but then why would the star collapse to a white dwarf? Why would the star's gravitational attraction increase without any corresponding increase in mass?

The accepted view of the birth of our universe is described in the big bang theory. At the outset, all matter had coalesced and exploded. What caused it to coalesce? The only logical answer is the universal attractive force of gravity but it is known only as a weak force unless there is something more going on.

What if the force exerted by gravity is not a constant function of mass as has been assumed? What if it is in fact variable? What if gravity's behavior is polar in nature and as stars degenerate to their lowest energy state gravity is able to realign itself increasing its respective attractive force? It is my position that in fact this is what we see happening on a grand scale.

As cosmic moieties are reduced to lower, less chaotic energy states - gravity is able to undergo a process of polar alignment increasing its attractive force, gradually consolidating material with other such pockets scattered throughout the time space continuum until all matter once more assembles for the next "big bang". In short the possibility exists that the universe does not die out like so many scattered embers of a fire, but rather becomes recycled once we accept the idea that the gravitational attraction exerted by a mass may vary over time.

Having accepted that the gravitational attraction exerted by a given mass may change — the next logical question becomes, can we manipulate that change to our purposes. Since mass is not consumed or altered in the exertion of gravity, it is potentially the ultimate source of clean, renewable power..."

excerpt from a whitepaper dated 1974, Arthur Phoebus

"I read your latest paper." Ed sat on the front porch in the growing twilight.

"What did you think?" Arthur probed gingerly.

"I thought it was very cogent, well considered and thought provoking."

"Really? That's odd. The reviewer asked me if I also believed in unicorns and bridge trolls."

Ed nodded, "I seem to remember people saying something like that to Copernicus and Galileo, only it was more along the lines of did they think man would someday fly to the moon or split the atom? But then of course, the majority of people at the time did believe in unicorns and bridge trolls."

"Thanks, I appreciate the effort but I would hardly number myself in such exalted company."

The two men sat quietly for several minutes as the darkness slowly enveloped them.

Finally Ed broke the silence, "Well I guess there's really only one thing to do then."

Arthur looked up, "What's that?"

"Prove them wrong. Prove your theory. What the heck, I'm not doing anything else this weekend."

"Be serious. You think two fellows puttering around in a garage in their spare time with no resources can conquer gravity. Are you crazy?"

Ed laughed softly, "I am both crazy and I'm serious. Look at Wilbur and Orville. I'm sure that people thought they were crazy too. Of course it will probably take us more than just one weekend."

Our story begins more than thirty years later.

1

The space somehow fit the moment.

Over the course of time the detached garage that had served for decades as the shop had become a rambling extension of its inhabitants. You had to wonder if the faded wood frame building existed to house the odd collection of equipment and junk or if in fact it was the contents that prevented the structure from collapsing. Hidden at the back of this maze amassed over the span of a lifetime, under the light of a hanging fluorescent Arthur and Ed stood staring at a small, black plastic box. It sat resting in the middle of the workbench among the litter of bits of wire, screws and tools. Protruding from a hole in one side was a round rod with a ring attached to a foot long piece of thin beaded chain.

Holding his breath, Arthur pushed the rod all the way into the box and took a half step back. Slowly a soft bluish glow enveloped first the box and then the surrounding clutter which began to orient itself and push back from the center. The faint smell of ozone grew and as the two men watched, the box lifted and righted itself. Rotating idly the black cube rose until it pulled gently against the tether. The thin chain resisted and the control rod slowly withdrew part of the way causing the glow to diminish slightly. As it did, the box reached equilibrium and hung immobile suspended between heaven and Earth.

Arthur finally managed to look away from the gently glowing box that hovered a foot above the tabletop and at the exhausted face of his brother-in-law, friend and long time partner. As though afraid to break the spell that held it, he barely whispered a single word, "Control."

Ed just continued to stare, "Thank God. I don't think I could patch the roof again."

2

The office reception area was a study in sterile efficiency. Arthur had the unnerving sense that microbes might perish here for want of warmth and simple companionship as he sat quietly on the small sofa. Like the rest of his surroundings it seemed that it existed exclusively as a decoration and was obviously never actually intended for such a purpose. Once more he quietly surveyed the precisely aligned industry periodicals that graced the low coffee table. He had already made the mistake once of reaching for what appeared to be an interesting title. The sharp sound of the gatekeeper clearing her throat caused Arthur to stop as he realized his folly. Just in case he might try anything quite so foolhardy again the stony executive assistant who blocked his path had given him a glance that would freeze beer in August as if to punctuate her displeasure.

On the other side of the room an interesting looking shelving system was built into the wall and enclosed in glass. It housed the perfunctory business awards and plaques describing different corporate hallmark events and various honorariums for charitable contributions. What was different were four very interesting and obviously very old pieces of stone sculpture strategically distributed throughout the case. They seemed utterly at odds with the rest of their surroundings. Although hardly an expert in such matters the worn and weather beaten artifacts looked Persian in origin and Arthur found himself wondering if someone within the company were a collector or if these pieces were simply the only argument that the interior decorator had won. A small brass plaque adorned each one and while it might have been interesting to see what they said he thought better of risking the wrath of Ms Doreen Adler who guarded the inner sanctum.

While Arthur was not exactly young, he was also not exactly dead and as such it was impossible not to notice his warden. The detached professionalism of her demeanor, the quick almost mechanical precision of her movements somehow fit with the polished metal, glass and muted corporate pastels of his surroundings. He estimated that she was in her late twenties or early thirties and extremely attractive. Impeccably dressed in a tailored business suit, just like her surroundings she seemed a model of efficiency. Yet one could not help but wonder for all her activity whether she actually accomplished anything, other than to keep the riffraff out.

The overall effect combined to make him feel about as welcome as a rash and as the minutes crept past and begrudgingly became hours, rash was exactly what Arthur began to believe his decision to come here was. Still, he and Ed discussed and planned what they might do when their breakthrough came and had long ago decided this was their first, best option. Frankly, it seemed to be their only option, at least it was the only one that they could come up with. After all, Ed had worked for the corporation for over thirty years and the company had a standing open door policy that was supposed to encourage employees to bring suggestions to management. It had been their electronic answer to the suggestion box of yesteryear. Simply email your request for an audience to present your new idea and everyone would be granted access. Of course when they instituted the policy they had probably not envisioned one of their plant maintenance supervisors and his crackpot brother-in-law actually taking them up on it, let alone insisting that it go all the way to the top. Although it had not been easy by any measure, Ed had politely but firmly stuck to his guns refusing to explain the exact nature of their discovery and insisting they could not reveal it below the board room level. When pressed he told them only it was a new and promising power source. The process had taken 8 weeks of memos, forms, emails and calls containing everything from friendly advice to veiled threats from both labor and management but begrudgingly the waters of middle management slowly parted and cleared a pathway to the company president.

So on the strength of all they had endured and in the absence of alternatives, Arthur was content to wait. One of the benefits of having grown up in an era of carbon paper and vacuum tubes was that the man and patience were not strangers. It seemed odd, this crazy hectic world that had grown up around him as he puttered in the lab and taught his classes. Civilization had prayed to technology for time and in its place, technology had given the world speed. Confusing the two was an easy mistake but it seemed the result was to see patience sacrificed on the altar. Perhaps that was why society at large always felt a half step behind. Arthur was immune. The disappointments of countless failures, decades of sacrifice and the simple knowledge that the answer rested in the small case on his knees was enough to quiet any doubts. So as the hours passed leaving his original "appointment" in its wake, he smiled serenely and retreated into the laboratory of the mind. After forty years of suffering the rejection and derision of the scientific community, he had not only proven his theories but with Ed's help had put them into practice and created a practical demonstration.

So he sat calmly as the parade of fortunate souls who had the presence of mind and efficient secretarial help to secure their position on the elusive calendar of Julius Wingate passed in review. Once or twice during a lull in activity, Arthur almost permitted himself to hope he would finally get the 5 minute interview he had been promised but that soon passed. Without intending to, he conjured up the image from "The Wizard of OZ" when the guard at the Emerald City brandishes his rifle, complete with flower and proclaims, "Not Nobody – Not No How" to Dorothy and her friends. Of course, they did manage to get an audience but somehow the visual of Julius Wingate as a gigantic head bellowing forth flame was a little unnerving.

Arthur once more patted the case on his knees for some reassurance and permitted his thoughts to drift back to Lydia. How many times had they watched that scene together?

Meanwhile, from the corner of her eye Doreen watched the new fixture in her office. It was intensely annoying. Primarily because the old gentleman was not, in fact quite the contrary, he was polite, soft spoken and patient. It was like having the Dali Lama sitting on the sofa. He remained calmly in his rumpled khakis, his jacket and tie had to be at least twenty years old and he could really use a haircut. The whole thing was preposterous. Damn but he was patient. She had explained to him that Mr. Wingate was extremely busy, three times. Mr. Wingate sent his apologies, but important matters had come up that precluded his ability to meet with the man. She would happy to arrange another meeting with someone else who would be in a far better position to assist him. To which his reply was always the same, "No thank you – that's quite alright. I understand and appreciate you are trying to help me but I'll wait."

It was maddening.

Nobody is really that nice. What was in that case he was carrying? Obviously it had gone through security – it couldn't be anything dangerous, could it? Maybe she should call security… but the prospect of several ex-linebackers tossing the old guy out on his ear was not exactly the kind of thing the company might appreciate seeing on the six o'clock news…

"Are you sure I can't get someone else to help you – I hate to see you wasting your day. I am sure that I can get Mr. Marsincko to meet with you. There is no telling when Mr. Wingate will be free. He has a very full calendar."

"That's very kind, but no thank you. I don't mind, really - I'll wait if that's alright."

Damn, she thought… what was this guy's problem? Couldn't he take the hint? Of course it's not alright but what can I do? He has to give up eventually. Of course the fly in the ointment was that Arthur opened his mail with a letter opener. Doreen opened hers with the click of a mouse. She never stood a chance.

Finally as the end of the work day loomed near, she gathered notebook and her courage. Giving a quick rap on the door and went in to see her boss.

Doreen made certain that the door was closed securely behind her and called out, "Excuse me Julius, there's just one more item today."

Wingate lowered the sheaf of papers he had been reviewing and peered over his glasses, visibly annoyed, "What item?"

She knew from her tenure as his executive assistant that she now had less than 30 seconds. Having resigned herself to this inevitability, she had been mentally rehearsing the explanation for the past hour. Doreen took a deep breath. "There is a gentleman who has been waiting to see you all day. He and his brother-in-law, a long time company employee, had requested this meeting through channels to present some new invention they developed."

"Oh… get rid of him." Wingate returned to the document in his hands.

"Well, I have stalled and delayed him all day. I've tried to steer him to someone else repeatedly. He simply refuses to give up and unfortunately, they are simply following your established policy and procedure. I don't know what else we can do without creating a backlash at this point."

Wingate dropped the file on the mahogany monolith that served as his desk, removed his reading glasses and tossed them carelessly onto the document. His tone did little to disguise his irritation, "We…WE…Don't you mean what else can I do? I have to finish this and be at my wife's opera club meeting in exactly two hours to dole out feeble smiles, mindless compliments and limp handshakes. Now you drop this in my lap. What do I pay you for? Can't you even get rid of a minor irritant?"

Doreen bit her tongue and waited for her boss to finish his minor tirade. She had been with him for three years now, long enough to understand his moods. It was odd actually. Sarcasm was reserved for his "inner circle". To everyone else he displayed an outward reserved charm, quick wit and analytical mind that almost universally seduced his associates, employees and the media alike. There were only a handful that ever got to see his darker side and Doreen was secretly pleased that she numbered among those few.

"Do you really have to go? We could work late again." Doreen replied in a tone that said far more than the mere words conveyed.

"Not tonight. In case you'd forgotten, my wife also has a fabulous figure – it's just that hers happens to fill a bank account rather than a bikini…and stop changing the subject. What's this guy's story?"

Doreen permitted herself a look as though pouting and repeated, "I told you, he has some new invention, for your eyes only. He and his brother-in-law developed whatever it is and brought it here. All he wants is 5 minutes. If he were just crazy, I'd have a good excuse to have security toss him out but frankly he seems nice and polite. I'd hate to do that, besides how would it look to have our guards escorting him off the premises when the environmentalists are still picketing outside?"

Julius had to admit (at least to himself) that she had a point although he secretly made a mental note that Ms. Adler was both using and speaking her mind a little more often of late than he liked, "Alright, send him in but tell him 5 minutes…and you owe me."

Doreen gave an all too knowing smile, "Julius – don't I always pay off."

"Hmm, by the way – what's his name?

"Phoebus, Arthur Phoebus"

3

Considering the transformation as Arthur stepped through the door into Wingate's office, his earlier "Wizard of Oz" analogy wasn't too far off. In the first place it was huge, it seemed larger than the small frame row house he and Ed shared. The furnishings were warm woods and earth tones, it was elegantly comfortable more like the study of a country manor house than a corporate office. He found himself surrounded by books, antiques and more art reminiscent of the few pieces he had seen in the case outside. It was as if he had been transported in an instant from the Museum of Modern art into the Museum of Natural History. Despite his long rehearsed elevator pitch – he found himself at a loss for words.

At that moment Wingate strode up, smiling and shaking his hand as if he had been waiting all day just to see Arthur, "Phoebus, glad to meet you. Sorry it took so long but unavoidable I assure you. Unfortunately I am very pressed for time, I can only spare 5 minutes but I didn't want to miss the opportunity to hear about this invention of yours."

The combined effect served only to further unnerve Arthur who stood for a few seconds collecting his thoughts again. Wingate was about his height but at least 15 years younger and powerfully built. The warmth of his greeting after his extended imprisonment in the frigid outer office had the older man's head reeling. Regaining his focus quickly Arthur replied, "Yes, thank you very much for seeing me and as I appreciate how valuable your time is – suppose I let our invention speak for itself."

With that he produced the small black box with its tether chain and a sash weight from its case. In a single practiced movement he depressed the control rod and set it on the carpet at their feet. Puzzled, Wingate saw the device initiate its telltale glow and said, "Exactly what is it that this thing is supposed…" He never had time to finish as the box repeated its performance, levitating slowly until the tether stopped its ascent by gently repositioning the control rod. The two men stood silently watching in wonder at the softly glowing object until after several seconds, Arthur reached out and gave the tether a tug like a hanging light switch cord, extracting the control rod. With that glow diminished rapidly and the box dropped quietly into the old man's outstretched hand. Recovering quickly, Wingate reacted like a man duped by some carnival huckster, "Wait a minute – what the hell is going on here?"

Arthur smiled, "It is exactly what it appears to be. We have learned how to harness gravity. Of course there are still various aspects relating to the practical application of the discovery that must be worked out but we have every confidence…"

Wingate cut him off and reached over snatching the device from the other man's hand, "Let me see that." He turned it over and over as though he might be able to see how the trick was done but the smooth black sides of the box revealed nothing. Arthur began to get anxious as he watched the device being manhandled.

"Please Mr. Wingate I assure you that it is not some trick. What you are holding is much more powerful than you might expect, please allow me…"

Once more Wingate broke in on the inventor's warning, "Allow you to do what? Perpetrate a hoax. Who do you think you're fooling here? More importantly, who do you think you're fooling with?" With that Wingate turned, device in hand and walked briskly toward a set of sliding glass doors that lead to a garden terrace. Once outside his powerful hands easily snapped the thin chain that connected the box and its earthbound weight. He then pushed the control rod in, placed it on the patio and covered it with a pail left there by the gardener.

Arthur followed closely on his heels imploring him, "Mr. Wingate, I assure you this not what you think and what you are doing is very dangerous."

"No…"Wingate broke in, "What is dangerous is trying to pass off some second rate parlor trick. I'm not sure what kind of racket you think you're working here but we'll just see how well it works when its wires are missing."

With that the two men turned and watched as the telltale blue glow enveloped the overturned pail, causing it to slowly rise. Instinctively, Wingate grabbed the handle that hung below it and held on for several seconds but his hand almost instantly began to tingle and go numb as though asleep. He barely managed to let go only to find himself falling about six feet into a flower box. It was from this inauspicious vantage point that he watched as the bucket, gaining momentum every second streaked skyward until it vanished out of sight.

During the course of her employment, Doreen had seen some bizarre behavior on the part of her boss, particularly when it came to his love of art and art of love but nothing could have prepared her for the next 10 minutes. Suddenly the office door swung wide. Julius and Arthur came walking out together chatting like long lost fraternity brothers. Her normally meticulous employer was covered with dirt, his suit was ruined, his hair was a mess and he was laughing about it.

"Now Art, you're sure that 9:00 isn't too early."

"Oh no, that would be fine – I'm looking forward to it. If you don't mind though, I really prefer to be called Arthur."

"Of course, silly on my part to presume, we'll arrange to have a car downstairs to take you home and they'll be back to pick you up at say, 8:30 in the morning. How does that sound?"

"Mr. Wingate, that's very kind but not necessary. I can hop on the bus."

"Call me Julius, and please we're happy to send a car. I'd rather it that way. Now if you don't mind I have a lot to do to make arrangements for the morning but I'll see you then"

As soon as Arthur had departed and Wingate closed the door behind him, he wheeled around to face his shocked assistant. His demeanor instantly transformed and his face hardened. "Doreen – call security. They are to put a guard, NOT a just a driver in one of the company limos and drive that man home. The guard is NOT to speak with him. After dropping him off the guard is to remain at a secure distance where he can watch the house unobserved. Also tell security to arrange for the guard's relief. I want a watch on that house 24 hours a day. We'll also need to have a limo, same conditions, there to pick him up at 8:30 tomorrow morning. Is that clear?"

"Yes Julius, right away…"

"Not right away – right now. As soon as that is done I need you to do the following. Contact Kang, Treavor and Van Dien – tell them to be in the private conference room for an initial briefing at 7AM sharp, in fact also tell them to cancel anything else on their calendars for tomorrow. Call and confirm via email. Get Chez' whatever the hell their name is and order breakfast for 6 people for that time and get me Hardesty on the phone, I need him here, now."

Doreen swallowed hard, "He's up north on the FabMet deal, you sent him…"

Wingate voice was as hard and jagged as flint, "I didn't ask you where he was – I told you where I want him to be, now hop to it. I have work to do." As he started toward his office, Doreen risked reminding him, "What about your wife's opera club meeting?"

Wingate looked back over his shoulder, "Tell her that Mimi is just going to have to die without me."

4

A few minutes later, having made the arrangements with security and the three other participants for the next morning's meeting Doreen relayed Wingate's apologies to his wife. To say that the call didn't go well would be a gross understatement. Mrs. Mildred Wingate was furious and so naturally the young lady was the recipient. After listening in forced silence for a few minutes, she offered a polite excuse of urgent matters to attend to and hung up. She did permit herself a brief moment to savor a "what a bitch and no wonder he cheats on you moment" just to get the bad taste out of her mouth. Then proceeded with the task she looked forward to least by placing a call to Hardesty's cell phone. It barely rang when she heard him answer the phone without speaking. Doreen hated it when he did that, "Hardesty are you there – pick up please."

On the other end of the call his she heard his emotionless reply, "Of course I'm here – who else would answer my phone?"

Exasperated, Doreen continued, "I just don't understand why you can't just say hello like normal people."

"Maybe that's your answer – what do you want Doreen? I'm on my way out to a meeting"

"Julius needs to talk to you – hold on."

Doreen always made it a point to refer to her boss by his first name when dealing with Hardesty. She subconsciously wanted to remind him that she was close to their employer, closer than he was. Frankly the man scared the hell out of her. There was a detachment about him that barely registered on the human scale. If she read in the paper that he had been arrested as a serial axe murderer her biggest question wouldn't be why he did it but rather who would leave an axe lying around with him in the room.

Doreen buzzed into the office and announced that she had located Hardesty but to her surprise, Wingate did not pick up the extension. Instead he simply gave her a message to convey.

Doreen released the hold button and relayed the instructions verbatim. "Hardesty, Julius said that everything else is on hold. You are to report to his office tonight, regardless of the hour and the boss will be waiting for you. He said rent a plane if you have to but get here now and don't ask me why because I'm just the messenger."

As soon as she finished, the line went dead. Typical she thought, no acknowledgement, not even good bye. After emailing the catering order she risked a knock on the door and a cautious, "Julius, I've made all your arrangements for the morning – is there anything else I can do?"

She stopped amazed. Wingate was seated at his desk, studying his computer monitor still wearing the filthy suit she had seen him in with the inventor Arthur Phoebus. He had not even washed his face or combed his hair. Wingate looked up, "Yes - cancel all my calls and appointments for tomorrow and one more thing."

"Yes, Julius"

"You never heard of Arthur Phoebus. The events of today never happened. You never recalled Hardesty, you never talked to security and you never booked the private conference room for tomorrow. None of it happened - got it."

"Yes, Julius – I understand"

"No, you don't understand because there IS nothing for you to understand. Now go home. Forget today happened and then forget that you forgot it."

Doreen wisely chose not to pursue the matter, simply said good night and quietly closed the door behind her while her boss returned all his attention to the computer monitor in front of him.

Before Hardesty arrived three and a half hours later, Wingate had managed to pry himself away from the videos he had been reviewing long enough to change into a clean shirt and slacks and wash up. Long ago he had a number of very sophisticated surveillance systems installed within the office. He wasn't worried so much about corporate security, he normally never kept anything that sensitive in a format which could be stolen here and there were numerous other countermeasures in place to handle that throughout the company. It was more to protect the trove of art and antiques he had amassed and had on display around him in the office. There were a few distinct instances when the system had paid for itself. Like the time that old letch Thompson had accosted his previous secretary right here in the office. What was her name again? Didn't matter, the video did wonders in facilitating that take over or the time those idiots from that start up web company sat here discussing terms as we listened in during negotiations. This however was by far the best use yet. He had three camera angles on the first demo and one on the outdoor experiment (he had taken the liberty of deleting the last few somewhat embarrassing seconds). Regardless, Wingate had watched each of these frame by frame so there could no mistake, no trickery – this seemed to be a true bill of goods.

When Hardesty arrived, in his usual fashion he let himself quickly and quietly into the office. Wingate was always impressed with the easy stealth and professionalism of this man. He moved like a cat. Wingate had once had one of his surveillance cameras moved just to try to catch the man in a slip up and still like a ghost he somehow managed to avoid detection. His face always seemed to be turned or half in shadow. Even his size and build were difficult to discern on a recording for some reason. It was when you met him in person though that you realized his most distinguishable feature was that he seemed to have none. His expressions were always deadpan, his eyes were cold and indifferent. Even when he spoke which was rare, his voice was flat, non-descript. Wingate had inquired once as to where he got his training but Hardesty simply sidestepped the question.

"Does it matter or are you really just interested in results?"

Without question, Hardesty was the best – which is precisely why Wingate needed him here now.

"I had to call in a few favors with a private pilot I know to get here. FabMet is all but sewn up. It was in the news. The younger brother committed suicide last week. Very sad – he was always the stronger of the two. John is ready to sign, you can name the price."

Wingate nodded, "Fine – good work… I can have somebody else sweep up those pieces but I have an emergency project for you. This supersedes everything else. I need you to devote your full attention to it beginning now. Take a look at this video. This occurred here in my office about 5 hours ago."

Wingate spun his monitor around and played the video as Hardesty watched emotionlessly.

"I assume this is for real or I wouldn't be here."

Wingate stared long and hard into that face across the desk trying to read anything there, "You assume correctly. What this video does not show is that 4 minutes and 37 seconds after this event a telemetry satellite almost directly overhead was knocked out of its orbit by "something", yet it suffered no collision damage. Nothing struck it. It just wasn't where it was supposed to be anymore. I got the NASA report. Here is a folder with anything and everything I have been able to collect on the two parties involved, Arthur Phoebus age 69 and his brother–in–law Ed Fisher age 62. Fisher is one of our employees so we have a great deal more on him but I need to know everything possible as fast as possible. First briefing is at 07:00 tomorrow morning in the private conference room. Is there anything else you need?"

Hardesty thumbed quickly through the folder, "This is a start. I need a secure phone line and terminal both of which are in my office. I assume it is still locked where I left it. I'll need coffee which I'll take care of myself. Who else will be in the meeting?"

"Kang, Treavor and Van Dien"

Hardesty nodded making a quick mental note, "Who else knows about this, at least internally?"

Wingate knew where he was going, "Doreen, a few people that were on duty from security, there will be a paper chain of those personnel who processed or approved the meeting. While they may or may not know that an actual meeting took place, I strongly doubt that any of them would have a clue as to the content of the "presentation". I made certain to have security start a watch detail on their house and warned Doreen against saying anything to anyone. She has always been discreet."

Hardesty took it all in, "I'll need the names. You know, just in case there are containment issues and I'll have my people take over for your security, limits exposure."

Wingate didn't want to know and fortunately the value of Hardesty was that he didn't have to. He knew that it would simply be taken care of.

5

By the time Arthur made it back down to the lobby, one of the largest security guards he had ever seen was standing by the elevator waiting for him, "Good afternoon, Mr. Phoebus. Please if you would wait just a moment, I have a car waiting for you sir." The guard joined him on the elevator and swiped an electronic key that permitted them to descend to the lower parking garage.

Although somewhat embarrassed by the attention, the inventor dutifully followed behind when the guard who ushered him out and directed him to a limousine that stood waiting. A second guard who might have been a twin of the first held the back door open and nodded as Arthur climbed inside. Circling around the car quickly the man sat behind the wheel and pulled silently away from the curb.

"I can give you directions if you need them, by the way I don't know your name."

The driver responded, "They had given me your address. For some reason the GPS went a little haywire just before but we mapped out a route. I'm really not supposed to talk to the passengers, its company policy and they tend to be very strict about such things."

Arthur sighed and sat back in the seat. This was nicer than his old recliner at home and he almost dozed off twice during the twenty minute ride. When they pulled up in front of 1342 Washburn Road, the car looked almost ridiculously out of place. Arthur found that the doors wouldn't release from inside and had to wait until the driver came round and opened the door for him. He thanked the huge man, who reminded him that a car would be waiting at 8:30 the next morning and ran inside to tell Ed the news. After Phoebus had gone inside, the guard made a visible show of talking on his phone while parked until his relief could arrive in a vehicle that blended better into the surroundings. Not that it was a bad neighborhood, but limos were typically reserved for weddings or funerals and even then they were not common. It was a typical collection of blue collar row houses. The homes were uniformly small two story and ranch style bungalows with neatly kept postage stamp sized lawns, hedges and flower beds. The front steps served a dual purpose both as a year round entrance and a perch for the residents in fair weather. It was one of those many remarkably, unremarkable communities where everybody seemed to know everybody else's business but still chose to mind their own. Yet when one of their own were ill, lost a job or a loved one – at every birth, marriage or graduation – cards, covered dishes and cookies seemed to appear as if by magic. Seniors woke on snowy mornings to find that their walks had magically been shoveled and skinned knees knew that a band aid was only as far as the closest doorbell. In short it was a nice place to live.

After quickly looking through the house, Arthur proceeded out to the workshop in search of his brother-in-law and found him tinkering with the backup unit. Ed looked up inquiring as Arthur entered, "Well, let's hear it - the suspense is killing me."

Phoebus smiled, "I finally got to see him at about 5 o'clock after waiting all day and you might say the demonstration knocked him off his feet."

Ed grinned back, "Tell me all about it…"

Arthur related the day's events to the smallest detail and by the time he had finished describing Wingate's soft landing in the flower box, both men were in tears laughing. When they regained a little of their composure, Arthur began to outline their next steps, "Tomorrow morning, they are sending a car to pick me up. They are setting up a meeting with a few of their key technologists. We still don't know what their thoughts are so I think it is wise that I go alone on this trip. They will be interested more in the theory at this point. If they try to press me on commercial matters I can get some feel for what their thoughts are but defer any comment until you are present. Agreed?"

Ed nodded, "Agreed – in fact, I am just going to work as if nothing happened. It will be interesting to see how that plays out."

Arthur turned his attention to the unit Ed had been working on when he came in, "What's the prognosis – any chance this thing will fly?"

Ed shook his head, "Yes and no. As near as I can determine there are some flaws inherent in the core so I wouldn't trust our ability to control it for flight – but I adapted it as we discussed in a rapid cycling mode to test your theory. Check this out." Ed flipped a switch, dials began to glow and their needles jumped.

Arthur stared, "Now that's cool. How much can we generate?

Ed shrugged, "With this prototype, we could probably light the neighborhood. Maybe half the city but with no power input other than the initial excitation charge and look, it's cool to the touch. No noise, no vibration, no fuel, no pollution. It's virtually limitless. Are you going to take this with you tomorrow?"

Arthur thought about it for a minute, "Let's hold off. We don't want to dump everything at once on them, besides we should be a little cautious. The power behind this technology is incredible. We need to make certain it will be used wisely."

Ed gave his long time friend and partner a sidelong glance, "If you want it used wisely why the heck are you giving it to people? Let me lock this up and then what do you say we get something to eat? I feel like celebrating – how about pizza and beer?"

6

Wingate settled back in his chair, closed his eyes and rubbing his forehead, said, "Give me the two minute synopsis on the players."

Hardesty opened the folder he had brought with him, cleared his throat and began reading ...

"Arthur Phoebus retired after teaching high school science for 36 years. The only child of a middle-class family, his father was a telephone repairman. His mother was a librarian. He received both his B.S. and M.S. in physics from Rutgers University. He had applied for a doctorial program but walked away from it when his father died suddenly from a cerebral hemorrhage. Instead he completed his teacher's certificate in order to help support his mother, who died 10 years later from ovarian cancer. That same year he met and married his wife, Lydia, a music teacher in the same school system where he was employed. By all accounts they were devoted to each other and remained together for 23 years until her death in a traffic accident. They had no children. Her only surviving relative was a brother – Ed Fisher, who I will address next. The keys to understanding Phoebus are his intellectual nature and sense of altruism. He has no vices to speak of. He has no sources of income other than a modest retirement pension. As far as we can determine his total net worth including the single family, frame home where he and his brother-in-law reside is about $350,000. He certainly isn't motivated by money but he uses what little he has conservatively. Doesn't gamble, doesn't even own stock. This discovery has consumed his total attention for years."

Without opening his eyes or changing position, Wingate responded, "Okay – the brother-in-law…"

Hardest was used to Wingate's behavior having seen it countless times. This was how he adsorbed information, concentrating completely on what was being presented. He continued, "Graduated High School then enlisted and completed 4 years in the Navy, honorably discharged as a Machinist Mate 2ndclass. He has accumulated over 100 credits attending a variety of night classes at local colleges and the university, but made not attempt to graduate in all these years. He's much more outgoing than Phoebus but still a loner by most standards. Seems to bear a distain for what he considers to be "educated fools" – much in the manner of Thomas Edison. It has caused him to have a few minor scrapes with managers from time to time. However don't underestimate him. He is both talented and extremely well-educated on a host of subjects. He is a voracious reader but likes to hide behind his blue collar. He is very intuitive and has an acute sense of the scheme of things going on around him. He is a very hard worker, extremely loyal and task oriented. Those are his defining characteristics. Like Phoebus, he has poured everything into this project and has less than $3000 in the bank. Never married but was engaged at one point approximately 25 years ago. Rumor has it that she broke it off but information is all third hand and unreliable. Other than an occasional beer and cigar, he has no vices. Needless to say, he is a direct pipeline to Phoebus."

"Good – next, our team…"

"Susan Van Dien…age 46, unmarried, no living relatives closer than a second cousin. Even her cat of 16 years died recently. She earned her first of two doctorates at the age of

24. She is both brilliant and driven. Very similar to the others in that she is consumed by her work with an important difference, with her it's very personal. She ties her sense of self esteem and worth to her ability to outperform her peers. That would seem to be the reason she left academia to pursue a career in the private sector. She is her own fiercest task master. The key to controlling her is control. She needs to drive. She needs to win."

"Next…"

"Kang Jong-kyu…age 27, unmarried, modest upbringing, he is actually a product of the foster parent system, his biological parents were murdered in a holdup attempt when he was 9 years old. He is an absolute software genius. He thinks in code. His track record in that arena is nothing short of astonishing according to his professional peers. He is versed in a half a dozen programming languages and his forte seems to be the seamless integration of multiple works to create unique solutions. He has no vices, unless you consider an addition to electronic and games gizmos a vice. He lives alone, no serious friendships or relationships either at the office or outside it. Very soft spoken, polite, has a genuine desire to please people and his work is the vehicle he uses to accomplish that. He should pose no problem."

"Agreed, now what about our remaining member?"

"Miles Treavor…by far the most colorful of our team. Age 39. Divorced three times. The longest union lasted 14 months. Where the others are married to their work, he just seems to like getting married. He routinely frequents the party scene, no doubt on the prowl for number four. Although he is a social creature and has a great many acquaintances, he has no friends to speak of. He is in a word, superficial. He is very fond of young ladies. He tends to drink a little too much and a little too often but he is not an alcoholic… yet. He has been known to experiment with different drugs du' jour, although amyl nitrate is his product of choice. He is an extraordinarily gifted engineer. Mechanical and control systems, design, metallurgy, composite materials, fluidics – he is cross trained in multiple disciplines, a real problem solver with a string of successes to back him up. He will make an excellent and malleable addition to the team."

Wingate continued to sit, slowly rubbing his forehead for a few moments then sat forward opening his eyes and broke into a thin smile, "Thank you."

7

Phoebus cleared his throat and for the first time in years found himself in the familiar position lecturing to a group. The major difference this time was that instead of high school students sweating over their impending SAT test, he was addressing a top flight team of some of the sharpest minds in their respective fields. Gauging his presentation to satisfy the curiosity of peers and still put it in terms that a non-scientist such as Wingate could readily grasp was always the challenge.

"Gravity is the underlying power source that fuels the Universe. Consider our sun for a minute. When we think of the sun we think of an incredible fusion reaction capable of supplying enough radiant heat and light energy to sustain us 93 million miles away, however billions of years before our star caught fire and the planets formed – gravity was at work and it will still be there long after our sun is a dead cinder. All other forms of energy follow the law of entropy and move to their lowest state. Radioactive materials decay, electrical charges dissipate. But gravity is not only conserved, it is additive. Only gravity exerts force without consuming anything in the process.

It is for this reason that I believe it is ultimately the single most powerful and important force in the universe.

In understanding our breakthrough, it is important to appreciate the logic that lead up to it. It began, just like the Universe, with the Big Bang. It has been theorized that all matter began as a compacted mass which became unstable resulting in an explosion of immeasurable proportion that created our still expanding universe. But where did this protomass come from? What caused its instability? It must be some powerful, universal, attractive force. The only logical candidate is gravity."

Kang broke in, "But Dr. Phoebus, gravity is an extremely weak force. The entire mass of the Earth is only sufficient to create an acceleration of 9.62 m/s^2."

Arthur smiled, "I'm a Mr., not a Doctor and what you say is true today but what if the value of gravitational attraction is variable, not constant? That was the premise I began with. If we assume that gravity was the driving force behind the Big Bang, and that the value of attraction as we know it today is insufficient to cause the compaction and subsequent mass to energy conversion required for the Big Bang, it stands to reason that gravity must have the ability to align itself and thereby exert force to a greater or lesser degree. As a proof of this, look at a collapsing star. As it compacts its mass does not magically increase – but its gravitational attraction does, dramatically."

Arthur turned and addressed Wingate who was looking very puzzled.

"In other words, look at our solar system for a minute. Our sun converts mass into energy in a gigantic fusion reaction that lasts for billions of years. The energy from that reaction goes streaming outward into space and it is lost. Therefore the sun must be gradually losing mass. So why isn't it also gradually losing its hold on the planets, asteroids, comets, the ort cloud, etc? Why haven't these things lost their orbits and accelerated off into space over the course of these millennia? I hypothesized that this was because as the star's mass shrank, its gravitational attraction was increasing, maintaining a balance. QED. I believe that this is actually part of the Big Bang cycle in microcosm."

Arthur then turned his attention to the three technologists in the room.

"It was this that caused me to consider the example of the domain theory of magnetism. Basically the domain theory states that a magnet is actually composed of millions of magnetic domains. When acted upon by an external force such as an electrical field or another magnet they align themselves along a common polar axis, and as their individual forces combine, the magnet dramatically increases the strength of its unified field. I believe that magnetism is in fact a specialized form of gravity in much the same way that a square is a rectangle but a rectangle is not necessarily a square.

Using this as a basis, I hypothesized that if one could determine the polar aspects of gravity and find a means by which they might be artificially aligned it might be possible to harness this elemental force."

Miles Treavor, who had been sitting quietly rubbing his forehead throughout Arthur's presentation simply could not contain his disbelief any longer, "Excuse me but are we talking about antigravity?" He turned and looked dumbfounded at Wingate, "Are you serious? I was asked to cancel my day and rush into this meeting to listen to some half baked theory. I can cite a dozens of reasons why this is utter horse shit. You have got to be kidding me."

Wingate visibly reddened but before he could speak, Arthur replied, "In the first place, the term anti-gravity would be a misnomer, better left to second rate science fiction movies. Gravity, like magnetism is polar. There is no anti-magnet. The polarity of gravity is more complex than a simple north and south but the basic principal of diametrically opposing forces of attraction and repulsion are the same. Second, every scientific advance began, to use your term, as a half baked theory which I think that puts me in some pretty good company. Third, these are no longer just theories. We have in fact proven these principals and have the data to back up our claims. So it would seem that even manure will grow roses when properly employed."

Wingate howled with laughter and called out, "Hardesty, I think it's about time for the videos."

The lights dimmed and the projection screen at the end of the conference came to life while the participants in the room watched transfixed.

Several minutes later when the room lights came back up, Arthur once more faced the small group, "What you witnessed was not a trick. We've discovered a way to control gravitational polarity. I realize that on the surface it seems farfetched but it wasn't that long ago that splitting the atom or space flight were considered impossible. Now they're routine. Billions of dollars have been spent trying to create a sustainable fusion reaction and one of the biggest problems facing the technology is containing it. The Sun and every other star contain their fusion reactions with gravity. I would submit it is gravity and not fusion that is the ultimate, clean power source because there is no matter to energy conversion. Nothing is lost. Nothing is consumed. There are no harmful byproducts."

For the first time Susan Van Dien spoke up, "How quickly can you be ready to demonstrate again? We'll need some time to design and prepare a battery of experiments to assess your work of course. In advance of that I'll need to get copies of your research for review."

"Currently we have only one functioning unit," Arthur smiled, "the other is…traveling. The one we have has been configured to operate as an electrical generating system. Rather amazing actually. It would take about 3 weeks to prepare another prototype engine for flight. We want to integrate some superior control mechanisms. While what we had worked, it was rather crude which is one of the reasons why it is probably already outside the moon's orbit."

Treavor broke in, "Excuse me did I understand you to say that you have a unit currently using this principle that is producing electricity?"

"Oh yes," Phoebus continued, "Very elegant solution actually. Electrons have no rest mass but because they travel at speeds approaching that of light they do possess a relativistic mass of .00055 AMUs. For this reason they can be captured by intense gravitational fields such as black holes. As the electron slows within the presence of the field its relativistic mass drops toward its rest mass of zero. By creating a rapidly oscillating gravitational field we can create extremely wide swings in the effective energy states of electrons within the sphere of influence of the generator's field producing tremendous amounts of usable power. I have hypothesized that this is the mechanism behind astronomical phenomena such as pulsars."

"Define tremendous," Treavor looked doubtful.

"Well," Arthur continued. "We have only run our little test unit at what we estimate is less than 1% of capacity and it produced 24 kilowatts – without moving parts and an initial excitation charge of 42 milliamps and 9 volts."

No one spoke for what seemed an eternity. Finally Van Dien spoke haltingly, "Could you please define little…"

"The entire test unit weighs four pounds when de-energized and it is roughly the size of a toaster. When fully energized we estimate its weight would be approximately 3 to 4 tons. We have to be careful to prevent it from cracking the concrete floor of the shop or melting the 4 gauge copper conductors."

"You have a four ton toaster, running on a flashlight battery, capable of generating 2.4 Megawatts of power." Treavor shook his head, "I've got to see this."

Phoebus appeared thoughtful and said, "Well that's not entirely accurate. The initial external excitation charge is only required to start the reaction. After that it no longer needs the battery, the process is self-sustaining. I can certainly make arrangements for a demonstration. With regard to review, I have all my notebooks of course and in anticipation of this meeting I had taken the liberty of preparing a synopsis in the form of a white paper – however, there is a problem."

Julius perked up, "Problem, what problem?"

8

Lunch hour had just begun when Ed was approached by his supervisor in the break room, "Fisher, get your ass in my office. I need to see you right now!"

Ed shrugged his shoulders and exchanged a look of disbelief with the other fellows on his shift but he replaced his coffee mug on its customary hook and started toward the office door of the partitioned glass cubicle. He and Sam Warner had been good friends for as long as he could remember. In fact it was Sam that had gotten Ed his job here in the first place.

He was nervously shuffling through some papers as Ed walked in, "Close that door behind you and sit down."

"Sure Sam, what's the matter?"

Sam looked frustrated, "The problem is that I don't know what the problem is. You've been here for over thirty years. You're the best man on that floor out there. Never missed a day. Did something happen that I don't know about? Did you do anything that would piss off somebody in management?"

"No, Sam you know me better than that." Ed looked bewildered, "What the heck are you talking about? What's going on?"

"That's what I can't understand, Ed. I just got a call not ten minutes ago from the VP of Operations. I've never even talked to this guy before. He asked if you worked for me and I told him yes." Sam hesitated, "Then he said, well he doesn't anymore. Just like that. He said you were to report to some guy in named Macelheny in Human Resources immediately. I don't understand, why would the fire you?"

Ed felt his heart sink to his knees, "Arthur, my brother-in-law, you know…he went to see Wingate with something that we invented. He was meeting with him again this morning. Gees, I don't know. Maybe the big boss wasn't as impressed as Arthur thought."

The two men sat silently reading each other's thoughts for a few moments, "I'm sorry Ed. Do you have any idea what you're going to do now? I mean you're a great worker. You're a talented guy…"

Ed cut him off in mid sentence, "I appreciate what you're trying to say but if I were as wonderful as all that I probably wouldn't be on my way to collect a pink slip. To answer your question – I don't have a clue. I can't afford to retire and I don't see anybody jumping up to hire somebody my age, but…" Ed stood up and smiled, "I'm not dead yet and I'll figure something out. Thanks, Sam – for everything."

Sam rose with him, "Look, let me see what I can find out. Maybe the Union can do something, I don't know."

"It's okay." Ed held out his hand, "I don't want to create trouble for a lot of people. You're all my friends. What are they gonna do - sometimes stuff happens. I'll give you a call later and let you know how I made out. Meanwhile, do me a favor and tell the boys they're gonna have to work for change. I won't be around to carry their sorry asses. I'd tell them myself but I really hate long good-byes. Besides, I'll be seeing you around."

Sam gripped his hand, "I understand. I'll take care of everything here. You just take care of yourself. There's something else going on here. I don't know what it is but it stinks. Watch your back."

Ed smiled on his way out the door, "I don't have to – that's what I have you for."

The others were engrossed in the mundane conversations and friendly banter that usually accompanied the potluck produced from a half a dozen paper bags at noon each day. They didn't see Ed as he slipped out the door and down the service corridor that lead ultimately to the landscaped quad at the center of the building complex. The administrative building was across the way and to the left. It was hot for so early in the year and Ed didn't exactly feel like jogging. He walked slowly up to the revolving door in the glass façade of the building, went inside and asked the guard for Macelheny's office. Following his directions, Ed proceeded to the second floor. The young girl behind the reception desk looked up from her computer and asked, "Yes, can I help you?"

"My name is Ed Fisher; my supervisor Sam Warner told me that I had to come see a Mr. Macelheny."

"Oh yes Mr. Fisher – we've been expecting you. I'll let Mr. Macelheny know you are here. Please have a seat won't you."

It seemed that Ed had barely settled himself on one of the small chairs lining the wall when a small, bald headed fellow appeared and introduced himself, "Mr. Fisher – I'm Macelheny; if you would be good enough to follow me please. I have something for you." Without waiting the little man turned and quickly retraced his steps back down the corridor between cubicles. Ed hopped up and followed him as he turned and entered his tiny office. Circling to the other side of the desk, Macelheny produced an envelope from his center desk drawer and handed it Ed, "Now then – you'll find your paycheck through the end of the week along with another check to cover operating expenses. Your pay records have already been transferred to corporate headquarters and of course in the future your salary will be issued from that location. I will need your old employee ID. Your new ID card is in the envelope as well."

"I don't understand."

Macelheny looked puzzled, "You are Fisher, Edgar A. employee number B3464937 aren't you?"

"That's me."

"Well then this is for you." He said holding the envelope out to Ed, "I was told that you would be operating independently on a special project and that you would be answering directly to corporate. I was also told that you would understand."

"I think that I'm beginning to." Ed said slowly shaking his head.

"Well good because I wish you'd explain it to me. I've been with this company for 27 years and I have never seen anything like this before. It appears these instructions came directly from the top and frankly based on my experience it isn't because anyone was feeling generous today." Macelheny stopped himself and turned pale as he realized just how imprudent his commentary might be but his concerns were somewhat relieved when Ed laughed out loud.

"Mr. Macelheny, you'll get no argument from me and I just want to say thank you." With that Ed turned and with considerably more spring in his step he found his way out of the department and back into the main hall. When he reached the corridor he stopped long enough to glance at the contents of the envelope and when he recovered from the shock ran down the stairs that lead out taking them two at a time.

9

"Problem, what problem?" Wingate looked up, "If you are worried about commercial terms, don't be. I can assure you that this company has both the wherewithal and the will to turn your discovery into a reality that can reshape the world and make you wealthy beyond your wildest dreams. I have already taken the liberty of making certain time and money will not be an issue in our working together."

Arthur hesitated for a moment then smiled disarmingly, "I'm almost 70 years old. Ed and I have no family other than each other. What would a fortune do for me…for us? Beyond a few creature comforts, my life is my work."

"While money in of itself may not have great appeal, certainly the prospect of unlimited resources to continue your work must." Wingate recovered, "Not to mention the opportunity to prove your detractors wrong. There has to be a tremendous sense of satisfaction in finally silencing your critics. To finally get the recognition you richly deserve."

"I'll admit to being human." Arthur chuckled, "But my satisfaction doesn't come from proving them wrong. Debate is inherent in the scientific process. The fact that I was correct validates a lifetime invested. What matters is that the end result has the ability to be the greatest benefit to mankind since the discovery of fire - inexhaustible, limitless energy"

The other four occupants of the room sat quietly listening until Wingate broke the silence, "Then what's the problem?"

"The potential for the abuse of this technology is staggering. I have no desire to see my work twisted or misused like Nobel or Fermi."

"Now I understand your reservations and they are very reasonable." Wingate said sympathetically, "but Arthur where does it begin and where does it end? You can argue that modern warfare would be impossible without bullets. Should we blame someone in Turkey for being the first to cast lead 6500 years ago? Is he at fault? Of course not. Since mankind began daubing paint on cave walls there have been two things that are unstoppable – the advance of technology and our ability to use it unwisely."

"Mr. Wingate, you are making an excellent argument for burning my notebooks."

"Precisely my point, you devoted a lifetime to better mankind – surely you must believe that the human race can prove themselves worthy of it…"

"Touché, Mr. Wingate but I need to see a pathway. This is far too important to trust to one person or group of people. Can you imagine what might happen if one government came to possess the ability to generate unlimited power, to repel or attract matter, to fly at the speed of light. It would be like a contest of nuclear warheads against stone knives."

"Yet, you came to me, to this company Arthur. You must have thought we would make the right ally in bringing your discovery to the world. You have to trust someone"

Arthur stood silently for minute, "Show me that you are that one. I understand there is no perfect solution but there must be a vision. A way to make the world at large safer, better prepared to accept this."

Wingate smiled, "Give me twenty four hours. You and Ed join me here, tomorrow at noon."

10

"Doreen," Wingate shouted as he raced through the office with Hardesty in tow," Doreen, here's a list of things I need you to do immediately. Advise me via phone as soon as you are done. Do not use email; call on the land line – no cell phones. Do not enter the office and do not discuss any aspect of this with anyone. This is a strict need to know project. When you are done, do not start a file – no archival copy is to be keep, shred the paper I just handed you. Oh yes, and cancel all my appointments for the balance of the week. If anyone presses you tell them I'm sick, nothing serious but I won't be in until Monday."

With that the two men vanished through the office door and she heard the lock click shut.

Doreen simply watched in shocked surprise. Of course, in retrospect if she had managed to get a word in edgewise it probably would have been ugly. As erratically as her boss was behaving, it could only have gone badly. Over the past three years, she had come to know his idiosyncrasies well but his actions over the past 24 hours had been way beyond anything she had ever witnessed. Doreen sighed and turned her attention to the list of action items in her hand. None of it seemed to make any sense, changes in personnel reassignments, material requisitions, authorizations, travel arrangements. All of it appeared completely unrelated, yet the existence of one list and Julius's insistence that no record be kept easily convinced her that not only were these things related but that whatever they were related to was huge…and all of it seemed to stem from Mr. Arthur Phoebus.

She quickly set about moving methodically through the list point by point. Nothing in her phone manner or tone betrayed the fact that anything was unusual. After completing the action points, she continued on through her bosses calendar cancelling and rescheduling appointments while deflecting undue attention.

Once she finished entering the calendar revisions, she carefully slipped Wingate's hand written notes into her purse and substituted a blank yellow page with her notes before feeding the pile through the shredder. Then before reporting back to her boss she made a quick visit to the ladies room in order to hide the document inside her dress. Returning to her desk, she buzzed Julius on the intercom, "Julius, everything has been taken care of. The action list has been implemented via phone and shredded along with any notes. Your calendar has been reset and posted for your review. Is there anything else you need?"

She stood staring at the phone, waiting for a reply, "No problems, you're sure that there are no notes remaining..."

"Wilkes in accounting was a little put out, but nothing I couldn't handle. Everything is exactly as you requested."

"Good...go home, thanks for your help. I'll see you in the morning." The intercom clicked off.

Doreen stood there for a few seconds staring at the phone consol in disbelief. She had spent three years at his beck and call. She had done everything for him, everything! Now here he was treating her like an old shoe. Doreen's hand involuntarily brushed across her dress where she had the folded paper securely tucked into her waist band. Until this moment, she wasn't certain what possessed her to defy Wingate's instructions with regard to his list. Now she knew. This was her insurance policy. She might not know exactly what was going on, but it all stemmed from the appearance of Arthur Phoebus and this list had something to do with it.

When she arrived at her apartment almost 30 minutes later Doreen made certain to bolt the door and draw her shades tightly. Then removing the carefully folded piece of paper she considered what best to do with it. She was afraid without necessarily understanding why, part of her kept saying just get rid of it, shred it burn it. Wingate was a powerful man and she had worked with him long enough to appreciate just how ruthless he could be. By defying him in such an outright fashion she was placing herself directly in the path of his anger but so what? Things had cooled somewhat over the past six months, become more habit than passion. There were no more illusions. In her heart, Doreen knew that that would always be someone younger, compliant and willing but then as long as she was being honest with herself, three years ago that had been her. It was only a question of time before Julius tired of a steady diet and began to look around again. If she had ever been foolish enough to think he would ever change, it was fairly obvious she was only kidding herself. Without some means to leverage her position she was powerless and she hated the thought of that. She had given him anything and everything without question or reservation and now for some reason she couldn't comprehend her world had been turned upside down. Somehow everything been changed by the unexpected appearance of that old guy, Phoebus. Her fall from favor was somehow tied to him. Doreen figured that she had about a year left at the top, maybe even two. She took care of herself, worked out, ran. She was in great shape. She had worked hard for this and wasn't about to sit idly by and let this happen but there didn't seem to be anything she could do. Now suddenly, her ever careful boss had dropped the very tool she needed right in her lap. Why should she destroy it? She kept tuning the paper over and over in her hands, folding and unfolding it.

Then she took the paper and sealing it in a plastic bag, she took it into the bathroom and slipped it into a small gap behind the medicine cabinet.

She closed the cabinet door and stood for just a moment staring at her reflection in the mirror as a slight smile crept across her face, "Thanks Julius."

Meanwhile behind locked doors at the office, Wingate was busy mapping his next steps and periodically asking questions of or providing direction to tight lipped companion. Small talk had never been a problem with Hardesty. That was one of the traits that Wingate appreciated in the man. It was impossible to like him, he would never allow anyone to get that close but you also could not help but marvel at his efficiency. His ability to obtain detailed information was staggering. He seemed to have a knack for finding out anything about anyone. Naturally, he guarded his sources carefully but Wingate had always found the speed and accuracy of his data impeccable. Beyond that, Hardesty was able to cut straight to the heart of a matter and rapidly lay out options and solutions. He had an uncanny ability to foresee reactions and consequences. With the smallest amount of directions – he took care of things. The company had a number of operatives to handle unpleasant problems but you might say that Hardesty was his unofficial vice president in charge of plausible deniability. As much as Wingate enjoyed a good game of chess, this was a man he had no interest in playing. Not merely because he enjoyed winning a good game of chess, but because Hardesty was not the kind of person you wanted to get inside your head.

Suddenly the printer next to Wingate sprang to life and began turning page after page. Julius looked up and saw the other man standing in front of his desk. "Complete dossiers are printing are on each of the involved parties to date with three exceptions – yourself, Doreen Adler and me. I have already taken the liberty of arranging transfers for two of the security guards on duty at the time. I had one middle manager fired and another reassigned. Your name appears on nothing. That fractures the chain tying you and Phoebus. There are other actions timed to occur in an apparently random fashion to further distance the two of you. Of your core team, Van Dien and Kang are loners, very adsorbed in work and should be relatively easy to isolate. Miles Treavor is potentially more of a problem. He is a lot more social, likes the bar scene and the young ladies that inhabit it. I understand that he has some skill sets that make him useful or you would not have chosen him. I have arranged to have him followed and lined up several, shall we say safe dates. Given the nature of the project, it was not something I felt you wished to leave to chance. Should it prove necessary, we can…adjust as needed."

"Excellent. Within 36 hours you should have lists compiling of prospective workers from a number of different locations on whom we'll need complete background checks. I am also looking to quietly acquire a property about thirty miles out in the country. I will probably have some hands on work that will require your personal intervention in that regard.

"Understood."

Wingate sat back in his chair, "Last but not least. You didn't include me in your research or yourself. Too bad, might prove to be some interesting reading. You also neglected to include Doreen, I'm curious as to why?"

"It is not a question as to whether to do something about her. It is a question of what to do about her?"

Wingate visibly hardened and his tone reflected it, "What did you find out?"

Before approaching the desk Hardesty had unplugged his laptop from the office Ethernet and had carried it with him. Despite the state of the art security measures he had built into the machine he was always wary of wireless connections. He placed the computer on his boss's desk, opened and unlocked it. Turning it around, a video of Doreen seated at her desk filled the screen. It had been paused showing her hiding the notes given her with express orders to destroy them when completed.

Wingate exhaled, "You're sure?"

"Absolutely, there is a complete evidence trail. We have her on video hiding it in the ladies room, then again in the living room and bathroom of the apartment. No question."

"Is she working for someone?"

"It would appear not, we are scrutinizing all means of communication. She hasn't had an opportunity to contact anyone nor has she made any effort to do so. The fact that she went to such pains to hide it would tend to infer that she saw this as some form of insurance to hold over your head."

"That bitch. After all I've done for her…", then lowering his voice," She doesn't have anything else put away?"

Hardesty replied in his very matter of fact manner, "No, we've had an eye on her for over three and a half years. There's no evidence of anything until now."

"But she's only been my assistant for three years?"

"Just watching out for your interests, Mr. Wingate – that's what I'm hired to do."

Julius allowed himself a dry chuckle, "Well, I assume then that you already have a replacement in mind."

"Her name is Ingrid Edlesen. She has been with the company for 12 years, 58 year old widowed grandmother of twin boys. Very efficient and precisely the type of person designed to put Mr. Phoebus at ease."

Wingate pursed his lips, "You're right of course. Make the arrangements and with regard to Doreen, I trust you will be discreet. We can't unpleasant intrusions right now. I don't suppose that you could arrange for her permanent departure in such a way that she could for all intents and purposes…vanish."

Hardesty paused a moment and said, "She doesn't have any immediate family or close friends - I'll see what I can do."

11

That evening across town, Arthur and Ed sat quietly in the tiny backyard of the frame house they had occupied together for years. It was now growing darker it seemed by the minute, cicadas were furnishing the music. The ancient, battered charcoal grill that had earlier furnished up the best steaks they had in years was still glowing warmly matched by the tip of Ed's cigar which seemed to float about when he gestured in the course of their conversation.

At Arthur's insistence, Ed had just finished describing the events of his day in excruciating detail. He ended with the look on the bank teller's face when he stopped to make a deposit on his way home. "You have to figure I have been going into that branch depositing my check every payday for 16 years now and Marie's been a teller there through three bank mergers. I guess she never figured I'd waltz in with something like that."

"What did you tell her?"

"Now that's where it gets interesting. The envelope they handed me had the two checks, a note and a new ID card for me and one for you. The note explained that for security reasons on the project, how about that – we're a project – the check was drawn in an odd amount. It said that if anyone were to question it, I was to say that it was a settlement check on a retirement fund. By the way with these new ID's you can walk right through security without the normal screening process. That way you can hand carry parts and such without having some guard inspecting them."

Arthur sighed thoughtfully, "This is what is disturbing me though. All this cloak and dagger stuff. Sometimes I think we should simply publish everything on the Internet and walk away."

Ed stopped and stared, "Arthur, I understand your reservations but you can't walk around trying to carry the weight of the world on your shoulders.. Nobody knows what you think better than I do but if we walked away now, there would be absolutely no controls on this. You know that. We need a strong partner to help us. What is it you said about unlimited, cheap, clean power?"

"I know, I said that it could free mankind from his insane quarrels over oil. Quarrels that begin by throwing threats and insults and end by throwing dynamite or worse…"

Ed stared at the glowing end of his cigar for a minute then spoke again softly, "As I see it – there are only three choices here. As you say, throw it out on the Internet and walk away hoping for the best. Frankly – given the human race's track record with technology, I don't think that's a good plan. Two, we burn down the garage, give back the money, change our names and move as far away as we can. I think we're a little old for that and who's to say that somebody two garages down the street isn't close to making the same break through. Or three, we do what we're doing. We team up with someone that can see your vision and will help us to make it a reality. I vote for number three. At least these guys believe in it enough to write a check and I'll be honest - that was a damn good steak. I wouldn't mind eating a few more while I still have my own teeth."

Arthur allowed himself a dry chuckle, "I'm sorry Ed. I know you're right. Good Lord we've been living hand to mouth for years. You've put up with an awful lot following my crazy lead."

"Oh it's not that crazy. I mean, it works. Think about it. Two screwballs in a backyard workshop come up with the single biggest advance since fire. If all else fails we could sell the story to the tabloids. They'd squeeze it in between the giant alligators in the sewers and the three headed, flying snake. Our story is almost as believable."

Arthur was smiling now, "I hadn't thought of that. I guess that would be option four."

Now it was Ed's turn to become a little more serious, "Well, you've still only given me bits and pieces of your meeting. Fill in a few of the blanks for me. Exactly what do you need me to do for tomorrow. Who's going to be there? What do they expect from us? What should we expect from them?"

"We need to bring the generator. They want to run a few tests but I am not prepared to leave it. That might prove a little too tempting. I am certain that Julius Wingate will be there of course. There were four of his people in the meeting today. At least three of them were technical, two men and a woman. Their names were Treavor, Kang and Van Dien respectively. The other person in the room was a fellow named Hardesty. I have no idea where he fits in all this but he seems to be Wingate's assistant of some sort. As far as what they expect from us, I would have to say it would be a functioning system where they could satisfy their curiosity by documenting reproducible results. Which leaves the operative question; what do we want from them?"

Arthur sat quietly for a minute, and then he began again, "I spoke to Mr. Wingate at length about my concerns over the misuse of our discovery, the enormous potential of virtually unlimited cheap power and what it might do both good and bad. Actually he seemed genuinely sympathetic and much more reasonable than I thought he would be. I asked him to show us, to show me a pathway to help keep this and all of us safe… at least, safer. It's a tall order but I don't know what else to do."

Ed who had been listening patiently asked the obvious question, "What if he can't come up with a satisfactory answer? What if no one can? What do we do then - roll the dice and hope for the best?"

Now that Arthur's greatest fear was finally out in the open, he felt an odd sense of relief, "I have absolutely no idea."

"Okay then, let me ask you a question. Do you think man is basically good or evil?"

"Well mankind has the capacity for both."

Ed looked Arthur in the eye and said, "Nice try, but that didn't answer my question. Is man basically good or basically evil?"

Arthur sighed, "I believe in the inherent goodness of people. If that were not so we would have long ago destroyed each other. It is easy to understand how evil can be returned for evil…and there is certainly more than enough evidence that a person can respond badly, selfishly, even destructively toward others even when treated with kindness and generosity…But the fact that "good" can be returned for "evil" defies logic.

The fact that we as a species can even over-ride self preservation to save and nurture others tips the balance. I would have to say that "good" wins."

"Then, I think you have your answer."

"I guess I do, but I still hope that they come up with something."

12

Julius smiled broadly as Ed and Arthur came through the door, "Good morning, Gentlemen."

This was Arthur's second visit to the inner sanctum and so he was far better prepared to respond to the warm reception. "Yes, hello again, Mr. Wingate – I don't believe that you have had the opportunity to meet my partner Ed Fisher." Never having been in the cavernous museum that served as Wingate's private office Ed was still trying to get his bearings but managed to nod, mumble a hello and shook hands politely. Wingate's firm grip surprised him a little and shocked him into the moment.

"I notice that you have a new secretary."

Wingate never missed a beat, "Oh yes, the woman that was here the other day was just a temp. I have been in the process of trying to hire a permanent solution. It's difficult because you need to find someone that you can really work closely with, wouldn't you agree."

"I can only imagine that the right person would be invaluable to an organization as large and complex as this one."

"Absolutely." Wingate smiled again, "Can we offer you some coffee, water, anything?"

Arthur and Ed glanced at one another and politely declined.

"Good, then let's get to the business at hand shall we. I'm certain you will be pleased with the course of action we've mapped out." He ushered the two men into an area in the office where a small conference table sat with a few chairs facing a large flat screen on the wall. It was only then that they became aware of Hardesty standing off to the side.

Arthur started to approach him, but the other man remained motionless his hands clasped behind his back. As soon as Arthur moved to greet him, Hardesty stopped him with a nod and said, "Mr. Phoebus, so very good to see you again."

Not wishing to appear too familiar, Arthur gestured toward his partner saying, "This is my partner and brother-in-law, Ed Fisher. Ed, this is Mr... I'm sorry...Hardy is that correct?"

Hardesty allowed himself the slightest of smiles nodded once more toward the arrivals and replied, "Close enough, delighted to meet you Mr. Fisher."

"Well, now that we have the pleasantries out of the way, please gentlemen have a seat and let me share my vision for a pathway to peaceful coexistence."

Manipulating the remote in his hand, the lights dimmed and the screen sprang to life. Wingate was in his element. Whether it was presenting to a board, the media or a shareholders meeting he had the ability to win the crowd. Public speaking came naturally to him and it had been complimented by access to excellent coaches and ample opportunity to occupy the podium over the years. He knew this would be the sales job of all time and he had no intention of failing. As the slides on the screen advanced, Julius began by describing the problem. Put their greatest fear on the table, nothing held back. Picture a world where ultimate power rests exclusively in the wrong hands. Reinforce the absolute necessity of preventing that at all cost. Get that first level of agreement. Now it was time to convince them that we are your allies, we also wish to prevent that havoc at all cost. Forgetting humanitarian reasons for a moment, we are a global company. The magnitude of the conflicts that ensued would ruin them. Logically, that would be the last thing they would want. Appeal to both sides of the brain. It was imperative to get heads nodding agreement by the time he reached slide 5.

He was almost at the turning point. What if we simply destroyed the technology, buried it? Wingate could compensate them but...what if someone else was co-developing it in parallel as they sat there? What if their intentions were not so noble?

Now it was time - Wingate completely changed pace.

Their goal hadn't changed. This discovery had the potential to improve the human condition worldwide but there was a major hurdle in the way. How to establish a "balance of power" and prevent one group from gaining an unfair advantage? They needed a way to dramatically and publically demonstrate the technology, in such a way that it was undeniable. Once that was done, researchers around the world would be clamoring for Arthur's work. Simultaneously making the world aware and universally providing them access to the science was their first best opportunity to seeing it employed peacefully.

The question was how to do it and Wingate had the answer. You couldn't do it via any kind of broadcast; too many people would think it was a trick. What if they built something impossible, yet recognizable - a flying saucer! Fly it around the world, over every major metropolitan center. No one could question the authenticity of Arthur's discovery then. In a single bold stroke, the world would know.

Wingate had the resources at his disposal - the manpower, engineering, facilities, and production capabilities, everything they could need. Of course they would have to construct it in secret. They couldn't afford a leak, but he had the perfect facility in mind to do just that. It had been a mothballed military facility just a short distance away. The company had acquired the property some time ago with the intention of developing the property. It was ideal, images of the buildings which were already undergoing renovations flashed across the screen.

At this point Arthur broke in with the one question that filled his mind, "I understand and I can see that you're right. This is probably the best pathway but there is still one huge unanswered question."

"What's that?

"What is to prevent you from taking our technology and using it exclusively to your advantage?"

"That's simple." Wingate replied, "You won't give us the technology either. We'll have exposure to it and to you of course out of necessity to build the ship but you and Ed can withhold any core secrets until after the event. We'll provide you with anything you need to build the engines, name it and it's yours. We'll handle the rest."

Arthur nodded thoughtfully, "You would still have some jump of other companies in terms of your familiarity with the process."

Wingate smiled back, "Give me a break. I'm giving you everything you've asked for. I'm committing hundreds of millions of dollars. I have stock holders. I need something to show them, is that too much to ask?"

Ed and Arthur exchanged glances and in that moment they both knew what the other was thinking. Ed nodded and Arthur turned to Wingate, "Alright, how do we begin?"

"I have prepared some agreements"

13

Thirty minutes later Wingate deposited Arthur and Ed in a specially prepared laboratory with his lead technologists from the day before, then excused himself and Hardesty. There was a tremendous amount to do while the others were testing Arthur's generator.

Once back in Wingate's office, demonstrating an uncustomary degree of curiosity Hardesty turned to his boss and asked an unsolicited question, "What was that all about? You have no intention of handing off this technology."

"Speculate."

Hardesty shrugged, "Your flying saucer would certainly create global panic. In the havoc that ensued stock markets would crash, tenuous governments would certainly be vulnerable. It would provide unprecedented opportunities to someone that was shall we say properly prepared… someone that knew it was all a hoax."

Wingate chuckled, "Not bad, even close but not nearly far ranging enough. Properly played, this is a gateway to global domination, both economic and political. We take over the entire planet."

Hardesty had to admit that he thought there was nothing left that could surprise him but this was over the top, "Exactly how do you plan on doing that with one ship, no matter how powerful?"

"I thought that might peak your interest. Based on what Phoebus has told me, this flying saucer could fly faster than anything in existence. What if this flying saucer was armed with enough tactical nukes that it could take out a number of major cities and military complexes within days, even hours of its appearance? It is H.G. Wells War of the Worlds but it's real. People would have no idea how many ships there were but there would be no mistaking the intentions of the alien invaders. If you think flying around would cause a panic, what do you think would happen when the death toll mounts into the millions and the planet's combined military is powerless to stop to stop the destruction?"

"I've got the picture but since you don't resemble a little green man, exactly how do you figure to come out on top in all this mayhem?"

"Ah, therein lies the beauty of all this. Let's further suppose that at the height of all this destruction, one person were to come forward with a new weapon capable of destroying the alien menace…a ray or bomb of some kind that could cause the flying saucer to detonate ending the threat. Don't you think that a grateful world, a frightened world, a world whose existing governmental structures had been shattered might just rally behind such a heroic figure?"

"You're serious…"

"Think about it. Throughout history every world conquest has failed, why? Because every tin pot dictator was trying to conquer people, subjugate them against their will. Of course people are going to rise up and resist. But what if the overwhelming majority were happy and willing to be taken over by the only person that can protect them from the Alien Menace? Even the paltry few that might object could never swim against that tide. Even in a worst case scenario – what you point out about seizing control by miraculously preserving our wealth and manufacturing capability for a broken world places us in control by default but controlling the fear of the mob, I truly believe that we can take it all. After all, we are the only ones who can defeat those godless aliens if they come back."

Hardesty expression never changed, "It's just crazy enough to work. There are a few potential difficulties, not least of which is what if somebody gets off a lucky shot before you hit the self-destruct button. I assume that's how your ray gun will work."

Wingate smiled, "Precisely. We'd need a self-destruct function anyway to prevent the crew from getting any ideas about going into business for themselves."

Hardesty continued, "Then of course there is the small matter of getting a quantity of tactical nukes. It's not exactly like they are on sale at Wal-Mart."

"That is precisely the reason that I am taking you into my confidence at this time, Hardesty. I know your work. After the fall of the old Soviet Union and the third world proliferation of nuclear weapons, I am fairly certain that without too much prompting you could secure what we need."

"I have a few associates that could prove helpful with the right incentives."

Wingate smiled broadly, "Somehow I knew you would."

"You might also want to consider some chemical or nerve agents. If we were to use those quickly and quietly first on some military facilities we may be able to seize some of their material and use it against them. Similar shock value – better utilization of resources, it's a Sun Tzu thing."

"You see Hardesty; I knew you'd warm to this project."

"In fact Mr. Wingate, you've given me an idea."

"Really, what is it?

"Well as had you requested, Ms. Adler has been retired. I realize you prefer not to know the details but in this instance I believe that there is an opportunity to turn this to your advantage."

Wingate looked puzzled, "Go on…"

Hardesty cleared his throat, "Last evening you wrote a note of sincere apology for your somewhat gruff treatment of Ms. Adler. It arrived along with several dozen red roses and explained that Phoebus (not his real name) was a college professor who dabbled in ancient Middle Eastern artifacts. In fact he had approached you with a unique opportunity to acquire a few extremely rare pieces for your collection. Due to certain disputes over the actual ownership of these items, Phoebus had used the ruse of bringing you a new "invention" to avoid suspicion with regard to his true purpose. The sudden flurry of activity at the end of the day was merely an effort to free your calendar so that you could travel to meet the old gentleman's partner and complete the transaction."

Wingate stared open mouthed in amazement. "I know better and I almost believe you. The next time I have to think up an excuse for my wife, I'm going to call you but how does this create an opportunity?"

Hardesty nodded, "I was just coming to that. In your note you then instructed Ms. Adler to toss a few things in a bag. A car would be waiting to take her to the airport. Because of the nature of the transaction she was not to alert anyone she was going, avoid phones. A company jet would fly her over to Abu Dhabi where she would be met by one of our locals. She was to check into the hotel and relax – you would join her as quickly as possible, a day or two at the most. The plan was to arrange to have all her identification, money and credit cards stolen. Any record of her employment here has already been erased. The apartment has been wiped clean, her bank accounts closed, credit cards cancelled and I have installed an operative to live there temporarily that resembles her closely enough to satisfy any curious bystander until she vacates in a month or two. At this point I only need to alert a few key contacts that an attractive, young, blond woman who cannot speak the language, with no identification or visible means of support cannot pay her bill at one of the city's finest hotels. She could in a word, vanish very effectively as per your instructions. No muss, no fuss and no inconvenient body"

"That's brilliant."

"Thank you but there's more. The explanation of your strategy made me think that a number of my associates, the ones that could figure prominently in the acquisition of certain items on your shopping list, serendipitously happen to reside in that general region. Suffice to say, it could aid our cause if I were to arrange for them to meet Ms. Adler. Think of it as a good will gesture. Of course in some ways it might have been kinder to have her killed."

Wingate shook his head and replied, "Oh well, I guess that we will just have to file Doreen under collateral damage."

"I'll get things in motion as soon as we're done. I do have some concerns about the money trail. Shuffling the kind of funding a project of this scope will need without unwanted attention from the board of directors…CFO's office…auditors will be impossible. I have no idea how much is in the Rainy Day fund but the acquisition of collateral material in the type and quantities discussed alone will require 50 to 100 million even with Ms. Adler helping out. Figuring in the construction of the ship the project could easily top half a billion. That being said, are there any personnel issues that you foresee that you might want me to look into?"

Wingate winced slightly at mention of the rainy day fund. It was an off shore slush fund that had been generated by some less than savory deals that had selectively circumvented certain trade embargos. They had been conducted with the full knowledge and assistance of some of Hardesty's government agency connections but there was no way to ever link it back to them. If it ever went sour, Julius knew that he and the company would be left twisting in the breeze. Any mention of it left him more than a little uncomfortable. The good news was that those accounts currently totaled over $120 million, more than enough to satisfy what Hardesty needed for the arms front and that would have been by far the most difficult line item to explain on a balance sheet.

"The board is my problem. The only two potential problems are Ferguson and Hooper. I can convince Ferguson to go along. With the rest of them in place Hooper can't do much to stop us. Harry is not going to be a problem, he cares more about fishing than finance these days but we will need to put the right firewall in place both in project management and finance. Both have to be at the top of their game and vulnerable only to us. Dig around in the dirty laundry bin – I'll need recommendations by morning."

"I'll get right on it, if there is nothing else."

Wingate waved a dismissal and turned his attention to a few quick matters demanding his attention before rejoining the others. Hardesty merely nodded and slipped silently from the office.

14

As soon as Wingate entered the room, the normally stoic Kang approached him excitedly, "This is amazing. We haven't come close to reaching its limitations. No sound, no vibration, no radiation, there is no appreciable heat rise other that the conductors taking off power from the unit. It's amazing. There is no fuel source. It functions more like an inexhaustible battery but there's no electro-chemical reaction and look at this." Kang pointed to a monitor screen, "We have been able to produce just over 1.6 megawatts, enough to easily power 60 or 70 houses, with no change regardless of how much load we put on it. Incredible..."

Wingate looked from Kang to the others and back again, "How much electricity can this thing generate?"

"We can't even be sure yet." Susan Van Dien's voice broke in sounding mildly irritated.

Wingate turned, "Why not?"

"A combination of the way this unit was constructed and the nature of the system's operation prohibit it. The terminals lack sufficient ampacity to handle much more load safely. The integrity of the overall structure is questionable and the field created by system is distorting a number of our readings"

Ed's ears perked up. "There's nothing wrong with the way that unit's built."

Van Dien pursed her lips, "I did not mean to infer you did anything wrong Mr. Fisher. If this is truly what it appears to be I am astonished you were able to accomplish so much with very few resources, however it is imperative that measures and controls be put in place for the safety of everyone here and the good of the project. The phase shift which occurs resulting in the radical change in mass…"

"In the first place, that unit is exactly what it appears to be and there is no change in mass. There is a huge change in weight because the gravity of the mass that's there is different."

"I misspoke but Mr. Fisher, these kinds of things are precisely what we are attempting to ascertain. However, because of the radically increased weight I have grave concerns regarding the safety…"

"Grave concerns in a pigs eye…you don't know what you're talking about. There's nothing wrong with that unit. Had I known how much juice we could generate I would have built heavier terminal wiring throughout but as far as the structure – what's going to go, the bearings? It doesn't have any bearings. Are you afraid the housing will collapse? It can't because everything shifts together – everything stays together. It could be made out of tissue paper but as long as it's all two ton tissue paper it doesn't make any difference."

At this Arthur broke in, "Ed, I'm certain Dr. Van Dien meant no harm. She and the others are simply trying to understand in a matter of hours things that took us years of trial and error to learn."

When Wingate left everyone was excited and guardedly enthusiastic. Now they were running in different directions, straining to be polite. Still this was to be expected and at least from one perspective it was good that the group was progressing through the stages of team building so quickly. Leaders would emerge, respect would be earned but in the course of that, periods of stress, conflict and friction were expected until the process would begin to normalize into a high performing team. That fact that they were already entering the second phase was excellent. He needed them working together at maximum capacity and they were well on the way. The best way he knew to stop them from concentrating on each other and getting them to re-focus on the project was to ask a relevant question, quickly.

"Ed, I don't understand what you're saying. Can you put it in layman's terms to help me?"

Addressing the question to Ed gave him standing in the group. He might lack credentials but that man had figured out how to turn Arthur's ideas into reality. Wingate knew that kind of intuitive mechanical ability would prove invaluable in short-cutting this process.

Ed smiled a little inwardly and replied, "In space, without Earth's gravity, astronauts are weightless but they still have the same mass. That's why when they get back they weigh the same as when they left. The generator has a deactivated weight of about 4 pounds. Right now, operating at this output – it weighs about 800 pounds, but if I shut it off it will weigh 4 pounds again. It has no moving parts and structurally nothing distorts because everything within the field has the same properties whether it weighs 4 pounds or 40,000."

"So let me get this straight," said Wingate. "If I understand what you are saying, the ship we are proposing theoretically could be made of anything, plastic, wood and wouldn't make any difference."

Arthur smiled, "Exactly. Because all matter exhibits the property of gravity we believe that virtually any kind of materials could be used and exist in a normalized state within the influence of a containment field boundary. However, just as a matter of course I probably wouldn't recommend paper mache as a building material."

Wingate shook his head, "Arthur, I know you're trying to help here but in English, please."

Ed broke in, "What he means is by using this technology you could create a selective force field around an object like a ship and completely isolate it. In flight it wouldn't even heat up aerodynamically because you could create a vacuum barrier envelope around it by pushing air away outside and trapping air inside. The ship would be like a micro planet with its own captive atmosphere. You could travel through space, with the structure leaking like a sieve and it wouldn't matter. You could travel a thousand times faster than anything on earth and inside you wouldn't even sense motion."

"Then, from what you're telling me if someone got scared and took a potshot at the ship…"

"It wouldn't even scratch the paint job. The ship will moves by repelling matter. It would be perfectly safe."

Wingate's face beamed, "Well I'll be…you know I was a little concerned that some trigger happy buck private somewhere might panic at the sight of the ship and fire off a few rounds. It's nice to know that until it completes its goodwill tour it will be safe from torches and pitchforks."

Wingate turned to his three key technologists, "Have you seen enough to agree that we need to proceed to the next level with all speed?" His question was greeted a solemn nodding of heads.

"Good. I should not have to say that this project redefines "need to know". The strictest secrecy has to be maintained at all times, at all levels. We are transferring the entire operation to a new facility under development as we speak. Susan, you are team leader. A project manager will be named and put in place within two or three days to facilitate your needs and keep to the time line. I need each of you to assemble and submit a list of any and all equipment you may need directly to me. Some materials are already being installed. Along with that we'll need a list of any personnel you would like to have reassigned with you. We'll do our best to honor those requests, the caveat is that that security and background checks will be paramount for obvious reasons. Any questions?"

Treavor who had been uncharacteristically hanging back throughout this process finally found his voice, "Yes, exactly where is this new facility and you mentioned a timeline?"

"In May of 1961, JFK announced that the US would land a man on the moon before the end of the decade. Exactly 2,978 days later Neil Armstrong was kicking up lunar dust. They had to invent everything, with little more than slide rules and coffee. I think we can do better than that. You have 8 ½ weeks. As far as where the facility is, it really doesn't matter. We've taken the liberty of packing you a bag. There is a van waiting downstairs. As a bonus, upon the successful completion of the project each of you will be paid the sum of $25 million. For every day you are early, you will receive an additional $250 thousand each. For every day you are late – I will dock you $1 million. Why are you standing here, the clock is ticking."

The three shot each other a glance and hurried to their respective offices to grab a few items before heading to the elevators.

Wingate turned to Arthur and Ed who had been watching the exchange and rapid departure, "I think they are all on board."

15

It was an un-meeting, one of those events that no one would ever admit took place.

At an Internet coffee bar, late at night, Hardesty and another man sat watching each other. You could not help to see them there without getting the sense of two cats, fur bristling, circling, unblinking.

"So how have you been Jack?"

"Why do you ask when you don't give shit?"

Hardesty revealed the closest thing he had to a smile, "Oh I don't know. Just trying to preserve the amenities I suppose."

"I wouldn't think that would trouble you too much, not after Panama. But then I never could figure you out."

"Jack, you cut me to the quick. Nobody got out of that one without a few scars but I didn't ask you here to reminisce, I asked you here to do you a favor."

"I fear the Greeks even when they bear gifts. What kind of a favor are you going to do for the agency and what's in it for you?"

"I don't want anything for myself. I just need a little time, 90 days at the outside to neutralize a problem that's all."

"Why should the agency give you any preferential treatment? Frankly, if you've got problems – good. Go hire an attorney but if you cross the line and any of our people get a whiff of it you might what to make sure we have a current copy of your dental records, for identification purposes. You know, just in case."

"Wow, that was pretty good Jack. You've been working on that tough guy thing, I can tell. Actually though, I didn't say that it was my problem. It's really your problem. Back on the 23rd it seems a geosynchronous satellite lost its orbit, yet diagnostically it was in perfect operating condition. If I remember correctly the report stated it appeared as though the unit was struck hard enough to knock it off position, propelling it outward away from Earth but without doing any ascertainable physical damage. Now if it was a meteor strike, which was the popular explanation, a hit that hard would have caused some physical damage and it would fall back to Earth. It wouldn't have been propelled away from Earth. Would it?"

"I'm not going to mince words with you. What do you know and when did you know it?"

"Relax Jack. First, stand down. I can tell you with complete surety, there's no immediate threat to national security. I need time to position a few things, 90 days at the most."

"There are other ways to find out what we need from you. If I were you, given some of the hard feelings in different sectors, I'd advise against taking that option."

"Jack, you really need to work on that hostility thing. Get out, do some fishing, maybe take up a hobby like needlepoint. If I were to become noticeably absent right now it might upset a few people, the wrong people. Remember 90 days, back off, a little breathing space. If you do that everything will be fine."

Hardesty's face and tone hardened, "If you don't, well I just don't think I could be responsible."

"I'll talk to my people. No promises but even if they agree nothing is going to happen without a very short leash."

"You know me better than that. I never could work on a chain and since the only way this will work is my way, I guess that just isn't going to happen. Oh and a word to the wise, don't try any surveillance, because you know that I'll know. Don't interfere and I'll be in touch or if you'd rather you could get a severe attack of brain freeze, do something stupid and see what happens but I wouldn't advise it. I'll let you get the check."

Hardesty almost smiled again and departed into the night.

16

Van Dien, Kang and Treavor sat together at a small round conference table.

Since arriving yesterday they had an opportunity to evaluate their surroundings. The facility was an extinct military base. Modular offices, laboratories and living quarters had been brought in and were in various states of assembly. There was a laundry, cafeteria, medical office, even a makeshift barbershop. Everything here was designed to make them completely self sufficient. Despite their protests they had been whisked directly to the facility without being able to pack a toothbrush. The security guard that accompanied them in the van had confiscated their personal effects including their cell phones. Everything had been bagged, boxed and labeled. After they arrived they had been issued light blue coveralls and directed to an employee locker room to change. Neither Susan nor Kang had been overly happy about it but viewed it as a minor and temporary annoyance. From the non-stop tirade Treavor directed toward each one of the security guards in turn you would have thought he was being skinned alive.

Finally Susan had quite enough, "Miles! You agreed to participate on this project. I suggest you get over yourself. All three of us are in the same boat but you don't see Kang or me behaving like some petulant child. While I may think the measures here are a bit extreme, I can certainly see the need for security given the nature of the project. It's only for a few weeks for Heaven sake. I cannot permit you to endanger our success so you need to make a decision right now. Either you get on board or I will be forced to speak to Wingate about having you replaced."

Treavor stopped as if she had slapped him. He knew that not only was she dead serious, but the ramifications of her statement were much more far reaching than simply being excluded from the project. Of course he would lose out on the promised bonus but he also knew that it would mean his professional ruin. Wingate would immediately consider him a security risk. If he "couldn't be trusted" he'd be fired in an instant and with that on his resume try finding a job. Or worse he'd keep "his job" and be shipped off to Lord knows where whether he wanted to go or not just to keep him isolated... Sure that was more Wingate's style, he would get him out of the way at least until the project was over then they'd fire him. Treavor had heard more than enough rumors and knew that the old man was a calculating and vindictive sort. He wasn't about to let anything risk this project and anything didn't include him.

"Miles, I'm still waiting for your answer."

"I'm sorry, both of you. My behavior was very unprofessional, just the shock of all this. It happened so fast. It won't happen again."

Susan pursed, "It can't happen again. We are on an incredibly tight time frame dealing with a technology we barely understand. Each of us is here for a reason, let's get started. While you were busy adjusting to our new surroundings, Kang and I took the opportunity to acquaint ourselves with the facility. Our employer is taking no chances; the structure we are seated in is a modular SCIF, state of the art so that we can speak freely. One of our divisions was constructing them for Homeland security under contract and they were diverted here. There are four such units on site interconnected through a secure communications network. All of the units and the interconnecting cabling are fully shielded against electronic intrusion. For security reasons, no exchanges of a confidential nature are to take place outside of these spaces. There is no wireless communication not even encrypted. No cell phones, radios, nothing. In fact, I understand that any communication outside of a SCIF is discouraged. The security force, which is more like a small army from what I have seen, is under strict orders not to speak with us. If you have a problem or question for them it has to go through channels. If it involves security – contact the shift chief."

Miles interjected, "So that's why that annoying ass wouldn't answer me."

Susan cleared her throat and continued, "That annoying ass was just doing his job, as instructed. Now, to the problem at hand. Kang – software, you are going to have to control this thing. What do you need?"

"I have already been giving this a great deal of thought. There are several existing software programs we can adapt from aerospace and military, principally in the areas of navigation, power distribution, systems control and the like. I can get several programmers working on what we need there without arousing suspicion. That takes care of the need that to govern basic control and information functions such as communications and life support. My greatest concern is…"

Miles interrupted, "Wait just a minute, what does this contraption need life support for? It was my understanding that this thing is not actually going to leave the atmosphere. For that matter, it should not have to function at high altitude."

Kang nodded, "That may be but I remember back to something Phoebus said about the unit trapping its own atmosphere. If that is the case, in addition to heating and cooling we will need to clean and scrub the air to avoid carbon dioxide build up. Fortunately that is a matter of adapting existing technology developed for submarine and space. The far greater problem is creating an information bridge into the Phoebus engine. I will require a great many hours just to understand how to manipulate and warp the fields to in order to steer. If this ship moves by selectively repelling or attracting matter – rudders or flaps in any traditional sense are worthless."

"I understand." Susan said, "Phoebus and Fisher are due here tomorrow. We'll all in need of a better level understanding for the purpose of planning. While the theoretical aspects are important, I'm interested in some of the practical insights that Fisher brings to the table. Given our short time frame any ability to short cut the process will be invaluable. Still what can we do right now to jump start the process? Beginning with a macro view, long lead time items and tasks first, what tops your agenda? For myself, I have already begun compiling a list of applicable modular systems. All of these are currently in production from different divisions of the company along with the project leaders who developed them."

"If I could get a copy of your list, please," Kang interjected, "I will cross reference them with my notes on the software side and also provide you with a list of hardware compatible with operating and control systems that I was looking at."

"I guess that leaves me." Treavor said. "I just have to build something to house all this that will fly through the air with the greatest of ease while looking like it could never get off the ground, with an engine and power source that are utterly unproven…piece of cake."

"From your cavalier attitude I can only hope that you have come up with an idea."

"I have more than that dear lady. I have a plan and a shell already under construction."

Susan and Kang looked at each other in disbelief and back to their co-worker, "Alright," said Susan, "Don't leave us in suspense."

Treavor laughed, "If Mr. Phoebus and his technology are to be believed than unlike every flying ship ever constructed weight and lift are not considerations. In fact, since it is powered by mass – it stands to reason that the more massive it is the better. Further, as it will be driven by collapsing and expanding energy fields it would seem that the simplest possible shape to control would be a sphere. A massive steel ball would also have the side benefit of appearing an absolute impossibility…shades of Star Wars, it would be our own little Death Star. Hmmm, I just had a great visual of Wingate wearing a Darth Vader helmet. But back to the question at hand, how could it be that I am already under construction? Simple, we drove past some on our way here, Liquefied Natural Gas tanks. Those huge, beautiful, pre-engineered, pre-fabricated vessels – we need only locate an appropriately sized unit under construction that can be diverted to our purpose. Voila, with the major headache of eliminating the shell design and fabrication we can turn our attention to the details of constructing the interior, again using modular construction techniques and we should be on schedule to complete."

Susan shook her head and smiled, "Miles, you can be a pain in the ass but I have to say at least you are one brilliant pain in the ass. That's inspired."

Treavor smiled back, "That's odd. I'm left feeling I should say thank you but I'm not sure why."

17

The security van carrying Arthur arrived promptly at 9AM. Ed had remained behind to work on the engine cores. In keeping with their agreement with Wingate, they would build the heart of the unit, keeping back enough critical aspects of technology until after the maiden voyage of their ship made its release safe. Arthur's purpose was to begin the process of helping the team to integrate the gravity engine into the evolving design of the vessel that would carry it to the world.

"Good morning Mr. Phoebus." Susan looked up as he entered the room, "can I offer you coffee?"

Arthur surveyed the room's inhabitants. Both Kang and Trevor looked as though they needed a shave. None of them appeared to have had much sleep.

"Coffee would be delightful, thank you. I am ready whenever you are to begin although it looks a little like you've already been at this all night."

The three exchanged a quick glance, "We're fine and yes we've already been working through a number of issues." Susan said, "In fact we have already initiated a series of tasks but we at a point where we really need some guidance from you regarding the technology. Where is Mr. Fisher? We thought he would be with you."

"Ed is back at the shop preparing what he needs to construct the engines. The actual process will take about three weeks. He doesn't have to be there every minute. In fact there are a number of tasks in the course of building the engines that involve waiting for materials to cure and such that do not require his physical presence. Whenever scheduling permits he will be here with us."

Treavor broke in, "How can he fabricate the engines without any idea as to the size of the vessel?"

"That's one of the elegant aspects of the process. It really doesn't matter you see. In the course of its field generation the engine converts other proximate matter to its gravitational state, just as one magnet will convert another piece of carbon steel into a magnet."

"Well how large are these engines then? " Treavor asked, "I'll need to design for them along with the means by which the ship can be navigated."

"Ed and I had previously discussed this at some length and we believe that the simplest way to achieve this will be not to have one engine but rather an array of small engines distributed spherically."

"HAH, I knew it." Treavor glowed, "I had already settled on a spherical vessel assuming that would prove the easiest shape to control by the manipulation of field energy."

"Excellent," Phoebus continued, "exactly correct. We were planning on a total of 509 gravity engines arranged with one at each pole, top and bottom, 24 spaced equidistant at the equator, with the balance of 480 units forming a geometric pattern radiating along what would be lines of latitude and longitude."

Susan remarked, "I find your application of global terms interesting very logical."

Arthur smiled, "Why not we are after all creating a tiny planet, aren't we? Each of the gravity engines will be a disc roughly 6 inches in diameter and have a de-energized mass of about 12 ounces."

"Hold on a moment." Treavor broke in, "Wingate wants something dramatic – which I can understand. We need to build this as rapidly as possible. For that reason I am looking at using a pre-engineered vessel, an LNG, liquefied natural gas tank to be precise. Now I've found one that has been fabricated, ready for field construction but it is 120 feet in diameter and weighs in at over 75 thousand tons. Surely we can't expect engines with a total weight of about 380 lbs to lift that."

"The gravity engines don't lift anything. They convert the gravitational polarity of the vessel and it lifts itself. It could weigh a thousand times as much and it wouldn't make a difference. This would be a good time to explain how gravitational polarity functions. We have all see in science classes the experiment where iron filings on a piece of paper align themselves with the lines of flux of a bar magnet. The North and South poles are clearly defined. The lines of flux are three dimensional but we only see a two dimensional representation on the sheet of paper. Gravitational flux would look very similar but it has no defined poles. It would appear more like the layers of an onion radiating concentrically outward from a core. This is where it gets interesting. Each successive layer is an opposite pole, for lack of a better term. The first layer or line of flux exhibits an attractive force, the next a repellant force and so on outward. We are used to seeing them in a relatively balanced state so that the net force exhibited is weak. However the gravitational engine selectively orients these lines of flux so that the net effect is either more attractive or more repellant."

Kang who had been listening quietly said, "This all very interesting but how do we selectively control it?"

"Again very simple, the engine requires a small electrical charge of excitation energy. Increasing the voltage increases the effect. Reversing the polarity of the electrical charge inverts the attractive or repellant force."

"Based on what you are telling me, "Kang countered, "controlling a single unit would be easy but controlling the array will be a different story. We'll need to create a matching array of gravitometers to establish a three dimensional feedback loop. Using this for flight will be a very complex software model and I am a little concerned about the lack of time for debugging. We have no experience with how these will react yet. I doubt you have any data on such an application."

"Yes of course I understand. We have played with three very small units running next to one another just to see what would happen. The fields create an interesting interplay but you are understating the obvious with regard to the complexity of control for navigable flight. The thought of a 75 thousand ton sphere hovering and turning could redefine the term system crash. What we have learned is that units can be used to generate a dampening field so that the action of one unit can be segregated from another. I have copies of all my notes on those experiments we performed with me for your review. I rather thought you'd want them."

Kang involuntarily nodded, "That will be extremely helpful. After I have had a chance to review them, I'm certain to have questions. Unfortunately because of our time frame we will be building the software before we have all the answers. The better our understanding the less likely we will be to make costly mistakes. How quickly can we have a quantity of the gravity devices to build into a micro-array for study?"

Arthur thought for a moment, "We should have the first dozen ready in 3 to 4 days which should be more than adequate for testing. As we progress there are some steps we can take to increase batch size and accelerate the production to keep us on track. The full complement of 509 gravity engines plus spares will take about four and a half weeks."

Miles broke in, "That's cutting it close. Do you have a drawing of these things? How are they mounted? What kind of power feed do they require? How is it connected? Is there any accommodation for measurement or control?"

"I brought along some hand drawings with dimensions that Ed prepared." Arthur said handing several folded pieces of paper to Treavor. "Each unit has 4 mounting lugs. To date we've run everything on a 24vdc circuit using a simple rheostat for control. Other than power feed for excitation energy, there are no connections. Threshold for gravitational effect is only about 6 volts and 22 milliamps."

Treavor took the papers being held out for him. "Amazing, I just gotta see this thing fly."

18

Ed stared in quiet fascination at the crucible that held the different elements which made up the alloy. It was odd really, after all these years to finally be here, in this place. The small vessel contained enough material to fill one of the green sand molds he had lined up waiting. Three molds, five cavities each. He had spent the afternoon carefully hand packing each one, cope and drag. Since he had made the wooden match plate, things went much faster but there was no point making the plate until they were certain everything was working.

His little homemade furnace was glowing happily now. You could feel the heat pouring from it even several feet away. There was something primitive about the forge, the glow of the fire, the heat, the smell, in this crazy, computer driven information world it felt almost like anti-technology. He liked it. It was odd in a sense, that mankind's oldest power source, the fire was helping to forge the next, yet there was something in that glow which spoke to ten thousand years of DNA and refused to surrender its claim on your gaze.

He slide off the stool, pulled his gauntlets on and lowered his face shield. Sliding the cover chimney aside, he poured salt into the glowing crucible to drive hydrogen out of the metal and reduce porosity. Then he reached in with a ladle, carefully scooped out some slag and then replaced the chimney.

Settling back he retreated into his thoughts as he waited. Waiting, now there was something that was almost extinct too – just like him. Just another twist of irony, technology was an opiate, addicting people to the crazy headlong pace of life today. The advent of labor saving devices keep people working longer, harder and faster but in the process –

nobody actually makes anything. They can't fix anything. They don't know how anything works. He remembered reading somewhere that Eskimos had over twenty different names for snow and today people must have over a thousand different names for impatience -road-rage, computer-rage, airline-rage... They must all be related though because they've all got the same last name. That was part of the beauty of this, the pregnancy of the moment. The metal would be ready but on its time and terms. Nothing could hurry it. Nothing could rush it.

He chuckled to himself. What was it about a fire that made everyone who sat and watched a philosopher? The dancing interplay of colors, the wall of heat, like moths to the flame...

He stood again and pulled his gauntlets back on. After fixing his face shield he once more moved to his little furnace. Sliding the chimney stone aside that acted as a choke on the top, he peered inside. He quickly tossed a small paper cup of sodium carbonate into the crucible and stirred it with a pry bar, then once more scooped out a little slag with his ladle before replacing the chimney.

Sitting back down on his stool again, he wondered who had first uncovered all of these techniques. He knew that the wash acid he had just put in would help in the formation of slag and improve the ability of the metal to pour but he had no idea why. There was probably some metallurgist who could tell him all about it but the thought of some ancient craftsman sitting by a hearth much as he was now going through trial and error was more intriguing. Evolving the secrets of his craft, holding them like close to himself like black art and then passing them grudgingly along from master to apprentice for centuries – that was the amazing part. How much must have been lost over that time? How many advances might have been the result of a miscommunication between teacher and student, wizard and adept? How many discoveries by promising and enthusiastic youth were seized, or buried by a jealous master?

His thoughts wandered back over his own life. That had always been his problem... ignored because he was "just a mechanic" until something went wrong of course. Then came the accusations and curses followed by the begging and pleading but in the end he was always the go-to guy, at least until the dilemma was fixed. Then he would be pushed aside, minimized once more until the next time. He remembered that time he had redesigned that winder mechanism. The way that bastard Hograve carried on I was afraid of getting fired. Then of course "the Idea" showed up with his initials on the bottom and he retired a Vice President ten years later because the line stopped breaking down every three months and me, I was just a mechanic. At least Sam was always square with him but he stopped making any "suggestions" for sure...at least until this one was ready.

Speaking of ready, he fixed his safety gear, moved the chimney and added his final ingredient. After another quick removal of the small amount of remaining slag, he lifted the small crucible from the furnace with his tongs and poured the glowing stream of metal into the waiting riser on the first mold.

Then he refilled the vessel with materials he had already weighed out to begin the process again and replaced it in the furnace. Once cooled, he would crack the first mold and clean the first five shiny little core elements to ready them for the next steps in machining and assembly.

While the next heat was melting, he carefully collected all the slag and material he had removed during the process. Placing it in another crucible, later he would melt it all down again and adulterate it so that his final concoction would remain black art, like those ancients he felt such kinship with. Like President Regan said – Trust but verify. If anybody did come snooping around they wouldn't find much of anything in the way of a clue. He made it a point to order and buy materials that had no purpose other than to throw inquiring minds off the scent. He had saved his jumbled collection of samples and failures none of which made much sense without him to decipher it all. The unlabeled boxes, bottles and bins held enough red herrings to keep a team of scientists and engineers guessing for the next fifty years if anyone had any thoughts of trying to circumvent them.

He sat back down to wait. He would break the first mold shortly, but there was time to sit and watch the glow for a few minutes. He couldn't help but think about how many times he had sat here quietly watching while epoxy set or metal heated, not knowing if this was the one that it would work.

The difference was this time, he knew.

19

Audrey ran.

To the rest of the world she was just a young woman getting some exercise as she cut down several side streets and an alley toward the park. Her long legs covered the distance quickly in a practiced, effortless stride. She had always stayed in good shape, but then she had to. As she waited for the light to change, she glanced quickly at her watch. Good, she thought, right on time.

Hardesty had arranged to have her briefly "replace" Doreen Adler and she had been in place almost a month. Both women were physically similar in appearance which made the selection easier. Her "job" had been to simply be seen around the apartment and neighborhood to confuse the timeline of her disappearance but that was about to change. He had used Audrey on several previous occasions for sensitive assignments and knew she was extremely capable. Her increased part based on how things were evolving could be critical to the success of the project. Normally, he would not have bothered to call a meeting, preferring to limit contact unless absolutely necessary but recent developments with some of his old agency contacts made getting a little insurance prudent. He watched from as she approached and timed his stride so that he would enter the heavily wooded footpath that wound through the least used section of the park. Once lost within the foliage, he slowed a pace and Audrey caught up to him. Together they turned from the path and started cross country. Once they were out of sight they slowed to a walk and after catching their breath Hardesty began filling her in.

"Sorry to have to change plans but we need to expand your role."

"I'm assuming normal rates apply."

"Hardesty shot her a sidelong glance, "Double.""

Audrey stopped and stared at Hardesty for a minute, "You have my full and undivided attention. What's the deal?"

They began walking again, Hardesty explained, "I need to divert scrutiny for a short period of time from a project."

"Scrutiny from whom?"

"From several government agencies, one fellow in particular – Jack Felman - You don't know him and he doesn't know you which is one of the reasons why this works." Hardesty held up a photo briefly for her to see, and then replaced it in the pocket of his sweatshirt. "Jack is not big on scruples and he is curious about certain activities. It seems we inadvertently disturbed one of his satellites and not knowing exactly how we did it disturbs him. I suppose that if I were in his place I might feel much the same way. He gets all bent out of shape about National security and other myths. Eventually when we are ready, he'll know everything but I cannot have him meddling prematurely. That's where you come in."

"What do you need me to do?"

"Simple, in your capacity as Doreen Adler you are about to be approached. That should occur within the next 18 to 24 hours. We are spreading a rumor among certain sectors that you are AWOL from your job as the executive assistant of

Julius Wingate while you contemplate filing sexual harassment charges against the old boy. Naturally he wishes to avoid any public embarrassment so everything is being held very hush hush. Officially you are just on an extended leave of absence for personal reasons but the pending suit is the real reason why you are not at the office."

Audrey nodded, "If you started grinding the rumor mill already you must have been certain I would say yes before approaching me with regard to the assignment. Just out of curiosity, any basis for the suit?"

"First, if I didn't know what you can and will do you wouldn't be involved in any capacity at all. Second, you are being very well paid not to be curious. Now back to the matter at hand. I have every confidence that Jack will approach you, either directly or through an intermediary within days. Knowing him it will be a full court press. Don't worry. If they attempt to pick you up for questioning, tell them you don't know who they are. They could be working for Wingate, or worse for me. You're afraid of reprisals. You have a meeting set up with your attorney and if you miss it, she is under strict orders to go to the authorities. That will get them to back down a notch or two. By the way, here is your attorney's business card, she is already up to speed but knows nothing other than you are Doreen and the story for publication."

"What next?"

"By the time all this plays out and they regroup, days will have passed. They will come back. They have to, moths to a flame. You'll need protection, assurances – you know the drill. Stall them off for three days, and then you can drop a hint. There was something odd that you recall coming across your desk that caused a lot of top secret activity and disappeared almost as soon as it surfaced. It had to do with some kind of a force gun. The technology was based on the work of some Romanian scientists during the cold war. That will make them salivate. By the time that comes to pass, we will have a mole in place that we can feed to them. Trust me – that will consume their attention. Then you'll be in the clear. We'll get you all the additional information you need through the attorney. You and I will not meet again until the end."

"When is the end?'

"After the hand off – you can occupy the apartment for another two months, and then vanish. By that time there will no longer be any need for any secrecy. If all goes as anticipated they won't have any reason to follow you. Even if they did Doreen Adler doesn't exist. Make certain they do not get your fingerprints or DNA by leaving samples of Adler for them to find. They will be chasing a phantom."

"Won't my running away make them suspect me?"

"No, get just get visibly nervous toward the end - tell them we upped the ante. Negotiations on the suit are breaking down; you are receiving threats from Wingate through me. When you run, they will assume you panicked that's all, just that simple. They won't dig any deeper. They'll go after the mole. After all, he will have been conning them for weeks. You were just a glorified secretary who remembered a name; you were duped just like them."

"Do you think of everything?

"Douglas MacArthur said chance favors the prepared man, one of my favorite little quotes. Time to go."

With that she broke into a run and rejoined the path on the far side of the hill, reemerging into the park and headed back to the apartment and a shower. She knew that Hardesty would wait a few minutes and follow a different path out. As she once more waited for the light to change, she unconsciously fingered the business card in the pouch of her hooded sweatshirt.

20

Wingate had been getting more than a little nervous before he visited the site. They were just over four weeks into project construction and it had been killing him to stay away, even with constant updates, video link ups and reports. He only avoided coming to prevent drawing too much attention to the site.

Thankfully, they were two and one half days ahead of the new, compressed build schedule in good part due to Treavor's brilliant idea to use an existing spherical tank under construction. In addition to chopping weeks off the project just in material acquisition and fabrication, the use of a vessel ready for assembly had created shortcuts in design. They were not starting from a blank sheet of paper; they were adapting something already there.

Seeing the vessel sitting there, with crews cutting and welding went a long way to help ease his fears. He was banking everything on this. Money was pouring out like wine but the troubling aspect wasn't the funds themselves as much as the need to disguise the real reason for the expenditures. Some of the monies were coming from an untraceable source, which was particularly helpful since Hardesty was using that to negotiate for weaponry that officially didn't exist. That would be a particularly tough one to explain away on a balance sheet.

But Wingate had not just been an idle spectator. He had been successful in ginning up the majority of the board for his "alternative energy" project. A video of Arthur's generator and the results we sufficient to convince the board that they were on the verge of launching a unique, proprietary means of power generation. They had no idea of exactly how it functioned but they could certainly see the potential. Powering a house from a shoebox using a couple of flashlight batteries was a pretty compelling argument, particularly when it was verified on screen by the company's top technologists as a true bill of goods. They saw it as an opportunity to print money and frankly they were a lot more interested in what it did rather than how it did it. Naturally, he had not relayed the true nature of the technology or his broader intentions. All of them were sworn to secrecy and understood the necessity of it, but it worked in their favor and Wingate's. He knew that they would use the opportunity to buy up additional shares. At least as much as they could without attracting unwanted attention. He could always count on greed. The beauty of that worked to his favor on several levels. It of course gave his voting block on the board more clout and it raised his share prices so that he had more of a market cap to deal with. Only two detractors of note remained to convince, one of them Julius knew would come around begrudgingly. The other couldn't stop the engine at this point. As long as the project was completed on time, everything would be fine but he could not withstand any kind of a serious delay.

Now he waited for Hardesty, who had gone to collect Miles Treavor from the work site and bring him to SCIF 3 for a private meeting. He would meet with the entire team including Arthur shortly but he needed a few words in private with Treavor first.

As they came through the door, Julius broke into one of his patented smiles designed to put people at ease, "Miles, good to see you – the project looks tremendous. You can't get a sense of scale until you stand next to that thing but my God, it's tremendous. Stroke of genius finding that tank but I am more than a little concerned that it really will fly. I mean – its twelve stories tall. It must weigh as much as a battleship."

Miles shrugged, "Arthur assures us that it actually works in our favor and frankly from everything I have seen in all our testing results I agree. He is a truly remarkable fellow. He's the real genius. He makes the rest of us look like rank amateurs by comparison"

"You are being entirely too modest, but then time is precious and I don't want to waste yours in some mutual admiration society. No, I have a much more serious reason for asking you here without the others."

"Alright, you've managed to peak my curiosity."

Wingate took a deep breath, "You must have wondered why I named Susan as team leader over you. She has a number of characteristics that make her very well suited to the position but I also needed to free you for something else that I have in mind."

"Go on."

"You see, I have not been entirely honest with the team for reasons that will be clear to you momentarily. I need you to appreciate the fact that you are the only one I feel comfortable bringing into our confidence."

Miles looked both puzzled and a little concerned, "Forgive but that sounds a little ominous."

"Let me explain. I will need you to install a few little modifications to the vessel."

"That's not as easy as one might think. The vessel has to be gravitationally balanced in order to fly and navigate properly. What kind of a modification are you talking about and why?"

"We'll need a tube with a hatch so that something roughly the size of a man could be jettisoned, like an escape hatch."

"Well if it's a safety and security matter, I can…"

"Actually it's not. You see, it's really not for people. It's to drop something else."

Treavor's voice hardened, "What did you have in mind?"

"Oh come now, we aren't children here. Arthur's fairytale notions of planetary brotherly love are not realistic. Once this technology hits the streets, all hell will break loose. The only hope for survival is to control it and that will involve a show of force. Nothing else will work and you know it. Hardesty here is already securing what we need to demonstrate our superiority but I need the right man, someone competent I can truly trust, protecting our interests at the helm. I think that man is you."

Miles reeled back a bit, "Hold on there. I'm just an engineer. I didn't sign on to fly this thing around bombing people into submission."

"Mr. Treavor, I think you are looking at this the wrong way. Because you are an engineer, permit me to show you the logic of what I am saying. I think you'll agree that once released this technology will prove an irresistible temptation to the wrong people. After all – limitless cheap power, wouldn't you agree?"

Reluctantly, Treavor nodded his head, "I suppose so."

"Of course it would. That is why we need to contain it, to save people from themselves. Not to bomb people into submission as you put it. Good heavens, you could fill that thing out there with bombs ten times over and you couldn't do that. But we can engage in a handful of surgical strikes on key military targets around the world, disrupt their ability to take advantage of the tip in power and discourage any retaliatory efforts. In short – it will buy us time. Following in the wake of that, we would bring inexhaustible, clean power - power to remake the world. Who wouldn't rally to our side? Would it incur some loss, absolutely – but it would be the loss of certain governments' abilities to wage wars using weapons of mass destruction. It's rather like burning out a fire break to contain a much larger forest fire. Ultimately, this is the greater good and you have the ability to play a key role."

Treavor thought for a minute, "New world order, eh. I almost hate to admit it but you make a very solid argument. Why didn't you start off this way, just tell people the truth instead of handing Phoebus that knowledge will make you free crap?"

"Actually what I am describing here is not that far distant from what I told Arthur but he would never have stood for using his technology to force the great military powers to disarm. The only difference is that here we are adding a preventive action to limit what logic dictates human nature will try. Arthur would never see that, but in time he'll come around."

"I wish I could find fault with what you say but I can't. Still I don't think I'm the man for the job."

"I know you are." Wingate smiled again, "Don't worry, when the time comes for that end of it your crew will know what to do."

"What do I tell the rest of the team?"

"Nothing – you just put in that crew escape system, as a safety precaution. Leave the rest to me."

21

"Arthur, can I speak with you for a minute." Susan poked her head through the lab door.

Phoebus looked up from the notes he had been perusing and said, "Of course, how can I help you."

Closing the door behind her, she began somewhat tentatively, "I need your advice with regard to...well, frankly it's about your brother-in-law."

"Is there a problem with Ed?"

"It's about his attitude and I am not entirely certain as to the best way to handle it. I thought you might be able to shed some light on his behavior that could help me."

"Really, what seems to be the trouble?"

Susan exhaled deeply and began, "It is not trouble, per se. First let me say that I have been surprised on more than one occasion by the extent of his knowledge in a host of areas. In fact I would go so far as to say that he surprises me just about every day. From a technical standpoint he is an irreplaceable asset to this operation."

Arthur sat nodding slowly, "Well so far that doesn't sound like trouble."

Susan closed her eyes, composed herself and started again, "It's the way he talks to me."

"Is he rude, abrupt or condescending?"

"No, it's nothing like that."

"Is he cold, impersonal or formal?"

"No, that's just it. He is entirely too informal. He has no sense of professionalism or decorum. I am in charge of this project. I received my first doctorate at 24, my second at 32. I'm named on over 100 patents. Now I understand that we are all living in very tight quarters here and I am trying to make allowances for that, but honestly do you know what he just called me in front of three of the workmen? He called me Cookie. It was like…I was some floozy were in a bar. The other day, he actually called me Honey. I need his help but I cannot have him undermining my authority."

Arthur sat calmly listening to her vent and waited until she was finished. "Susan, first let me just reiterate your comment about us inhabiting tight quarters here. You are exactly right and that does indeed tend to breed familiarity. High functioning teams become family, you know that. You should understand a few things about Ed and it may help your view of the situation. He is probably the most singularly brilliant man I know and almost entirely self-educated. The fact that he does treat you in the fashion you describe tells me something very important. You see if he was rude or condescending, it would be because he has no respect for you at all. If he were profoundly polite, it would be because you are his boss and he has no respect for you at all. The fact that he has accepted you in this fashion means that he considers you a friend, a peer. It means that he has developed a deep sense of respect for you and your abilities, in a remarkably short period of time I might add. The longer you know Ed the more you will come to appreciate that fact, earning his trust and loyalty is not easy, but it's worth it. So you see his actions, in his world aren't tokens of disrespect – quite the contrary. He likes you. If he didn't believe me he would call you other things I choose not to repeat.", Arthur chuckled, "He was in the navy you know. "

Susan pursed her lips, "I appreciate all you are saying, but it still leaves me with my dilemma. Because he comes off to the work crews as one of them, when they see him acting this way they think they can take such liberties as well. I cannot do my job effectively if he undermines my authority."

Arthur folded his hands and looked down, then replied gently, "I think there is a lot more going on here so bear with me for a few minutes. This is just the two of us talking and naturally nothing we discuss will leave this room. Understand that what I am about to say is only meant to help you, as you've asked."

Susan steeled herself and nodded.

Arthur continued, "Friction requires two objects working against each other. I sense a measure of insecurity in you…"

Susan started to speak but Arthur held up one hand to silence her saying, "You came to me and asked my help, please let me finish… Feedback is usually not pleasant to listen too. You can choose to think of it as either an annoying noise or view it as a means by which you improve something. What I am saying is meant to do the latter."

He waited a moment as he watched Susan relax just a bit, adsorbing his words and then continued.

"You push too hard sometimes. For example just a moment ago you felt compelled to wave your resume at me. There is no need for that. Like Ed, I have developed a great respect for your abilities. I am not impressed by your degrees. I am impressed by you, the person who earned them and your ability to apply your knowledge, your desire to learn and grow, your work ethic, your focus. I am certain you know plenty of people with PhD after their name for whom you have little or no respect. Am I right?"

Reluctantly, Susan nodded silently.

"As a boy it was not easy growing up a math and science geek. Certainly I know the abuses I was subjected too. I can only imagine that as a young woman it was that much more intolerable. People like you and I and Ed never fit the mold. It is odd to think that the vagaries of our society would cause genius to be treated like a consolation prize. But then we live in a world governed by beautiful people rather than beautiful minds. More is the pity, yet time has ravaged the bodies of the star athletes and fashion models of my generation while I still sit and solve my equations. Perhaps there is justice after all."

Susan permitted herself a knowing smile as Arthur continued.

"Ed's case was a particularly sad one – although he has never permitted his choices to make him bitter. He was a brilliant student by all accounts but when he graduated from High School his parents, my in-laws, had fallen on some very difficult times financially. He chose to go into the navy instead of continuing his education directly in order to help out. He was afraid to burden them. When he was discharged, he went out to work and although he used his GI bill to attend classes at night, without giving up his day job he found it practically impossible to pursue the course of study he would have if it had not been for his ailing parents. The singular benefit he derived was that while he was training his mind, he was also training his hands. The wealth of practical application experience he has accumulated is staggering. He has never regretted it, at least not openly but he resents what he calls educated idiots. I have personally seen his ideas turn up time and again with someone else's name in the drawing title block. You mentioned that you are named on over a hundred patents. Ed has evolved at least that many or more concepts but his name does not appear anywhere on the patent. There are those have literally made millions from the mind of that man. Yet he has never received the accolades or rewards he deserved, until now. I think that his admiration for you comes from a sense that in many ways you have fought the same fight for respect over the years."

Arthur stopped and studied the woman who stood across from him for a moment. Her demeanor had softened as she gradually began to understand the nature of Ed's behavior and some of her own.

"Which brings us full circle to the question of how to solve your problem without alienating this man? Here is my solution. Talk to him. Tell him exactly what you told me, that you have great respect for his abilities and although you appreciate his friendship, in order to do your job you need to preserve a certain level of decorum in front of the men. He has bossed work crew's for years. He'll understand without taking offense but I think you need to do one thing more."

Susan looked curiously at Arthur, "What's that?"

"Play chess with him. He loves the game and he is an excellent player, but don't let him sucker you in. That is one area where he is utterly ruthless, cold and calculating. Don't give him any quarter. Chess will provide you with an invaluable insight into each other's minds but it will also allow you to reciprocate the respect he has demonstrated for you. After all, you ask an intellectual peer to play chess. It will also permit both of you a forum to be friendly and familiar that is not job related so it provides an appropriate outlet. If a crew of workmen heard you joking about playing a game of chess, they wouldn't think twice about."

Susan shook her head in a small measure of amazement, "You know Arthur, I knew you were intelligent and insightful, but I had no idea just how wise you are. Thank you."

Arthur looked at her with mock disapproval, "Just don't tell anyone. If you give a reputation, I'd have to live up to it and that could be awful."

22

When Audrey returned from shopping, as a matter of habit she looked down at the floor in front of the door. There she saw a tiny bent staple she had wedged in the jamb before she left. Someone had entered the apartment while she was out and she would have to work from the assumption that they were still in there. Damn, she thought Hardesty was good. These guys were on time as if he had made an appointment for them.

She unlocked the door and stepped inside to be greeted by two men. The older, smaller man had drawn a chair up so that he was seated facing the door as she entered, the younger man was standing next to the door and behind it. Faking surprise she fumbled with her purse for a small container of mace allowing the younger man to overpower her. He covered her mouth with one hand and tossed the purse aside.

The older man simply cautioned her, "Please do not cry out. No one is going to hurt you. We are with the FBI." He held up a small wallet with a very authentic looking ID.

She stopped struggling and the other man released her mumbling an apology.

"What are you doing here? What do you want with me?" she asked.

The older man purposely kept his voice very calm and even in an attempt to quiet her fears, "Forgive our cloak and dagger appearance here in your home Ms. Adler. You are not in any trouble but you may very well be in some danger. We are here to help you."

"By scaring me half to death... Can't you think of anything better than we're from the government and we're here to help you? What is all this about?"

"It concerns your employer."

"Oh that pig. Why what's he done now?"

"That is precisely what we are trying to find out, Ms. Adler."

"I don't understand."

"Your employer has been under scrutiny for quite some time involving a number of dealings but there are few instances of late that have prompted us to step in at this time."

"I have no idea what you are talking about."

"Oh come now Ms. Adler, you were his executive assistant for three years. You can't convince me that in that time you were not privy to what was going on in that office. Please don't insult my intelligence by suggesting otherwise."

"Look I kept his calendar, got his coffee and took care of day to day chores. Nothing odd or unusual – at least not until he started to make some very unwanted advances. He has a very big problem taking no for an answer and now I have a very big attorney who is going to convince him in a very big way that he should learn how to do just that. I really can't help you."

"Can't or won't?"

"Take your pick and now you can leave quietly unless of course you have trouble taking no for an answer."

"Ms. Adler, we'll leave but before we do I'd like to give you some very sound advice. You are involved in something much bigger than you realize. I'm not with the Internal Revenue Service or some labor relations board. I'm with the FBI and we have strong reason to suspect that your boss may very well be involved in certain activities that are tantamount to treason. Not a term I use lightly. Now in the course of unraveling this mess, we'll be sorting out a lot of people, places and things – you might want to be careful exactly which category you fall into."

Audrey looked frightened, "You can leave now."

"Certainly," the man said, "but I'll be around – if you change your mind or think of anything you might like to share, my card is on the table. I'd advise you to hang onto it. You might need it more than you know. Oh and not to sound cliché, don't leave town."

With that the two men crossed to the door and exited silently.

Audrey watched them go, then quickly moved to the door and threw the bolt behind them. Quickly surveying the apartment with a practiced eye, she could see where a few minor things had been disturbed. She was relatively certain they had collected samples of fingerprints and possibly DNA. There was no way these guys were FBI. One glance in the bathroom was enough to confirm her suspicions, her toothbrush was missing, or should she say - Doreen's toothbrush. Perfect… she had made certain to leave out materials that would lead back to the previous occupant.

Normally, Hardesty would have had a clean out crew completely erase Doreen's past existence here, but he had held off since Audrey was put in place. She had been given strict orders to avoid leaving her own fingerprints and disturbing her predecessors in commonly trafficked spots like the phone. It was amazing how well Hardesty knew their tactics, but it worked. They wouldn't come back to collect again so she should be safe.

Since the entire place was probably wired now, she knew better than to dwell in any one spot, they we certainly listening in if not watching her every move.

She quickly crossed to the phone and called the number of the attorney Hardesty had given her then proceeded to leave an indignant voicemail complaining that now her pig of a boss had gotten her into some trouble with the FBI. They had broken into her apartment and were waiting for her. This was outrageous. Something had to be done about Julius. She was paying good money to get this affair settled and if they wanted to collect their fee they had better get busy and resolve this mess. She never wanted a repeat of what just happened. Then she slammed down the phone.

Turning back, she crossed to the table and picked up the card the man had left on the table.

It was adorned with the seal of the FBI and read Jack Felman, field agent.

She took the card, thought about it for a second and put it in the nightstand drawer. Then she quickly grabbed her purse and after looking timidly around the hall headed for the coffee shop to be in a public place surrounded by people as if she was frightened to remain alone there. That was after all what they would expect.

As she sipped a coffee she couldn't help but admire the efficiency of her boss. It was amazing, they were right on time just like Hardesty said they'd be.

23

Susan was not happy.

She walked into the small space Miles had been using as an office, a necessity in such tight quarters. Each of them needed an area where they could think and work undisturbed.

"Would you mind explaining to me what the hell they are doing out there?"

Miles swiveled around in his chair, "They are building a space ship. Pretty cool, don't you think."

Susan bit her tongue, "I am not amused. Exactly what are those men fabricating and installing in the base of the vessel?"

"You mean those things that look like tubes?"

"Why are we playing this game? Yes, the things that look like tubes and don't tell me they are tubes. What is their purpose? Why don't they don't appear on any of the drawings?"

"Now that's a better question. Remember the space shuttle Challenger or Apollo 1. They are emergency escape portals. Since no one has ever built one of these things before and people are going to be inside it, I thought it prudent to add them. The reason they are not on the drawings is that with all we have going on, I simply have not had time to get CAD to add them to the master assembly set yet. As soon as they were done drafting the section as a module I sent it to the floor so that they could begin fabrication of the three subassemblies. As soon as I can free up a draftsman, they will make the changes. Why are you getting all bent out of shape?"

Susan was barely containing her anger at this point. The combination of exhaustion, stress and Miles' flippant attitude had her on the verge of exploding, "I am team leader. This is my project. Before you decide to make a significant material design change like this, I need to be consulted. I need the basis of your design criteria, materials, manpower requirements, everything. You know the drill. You cannot simply reallocate resources because you got an idea. They had to be pulled from elsewhere on the project and that affects everybody's time line."

Miles relaxed sinking back into the chair and said calmly, "Alright Susan. Look I didn't mean to step on anyone's toes here. It was a structural design issue and that's my purview. My crews are 32 hours ahead of schedule. Because of the way they are designed, I can slip the modification in almost transparently to other work in progress. It wasn't going to upset other workflow and who knows it might even save a few lives. I just saw it as a personnel safety issue and took the initiative. You can't micromanage every little thing. You'll go crazy and take everyone else with you. Relax. We're all living on stale coffee and frayed nerves. What's really going on?"

Susan's blood pressure was slowly dropping, "You're right. Sorry if I dumped on you but in the future, if for the sake of professional courtesy if nothing else let me know. You are certain to need control functions and at very least interlock circuitry, so it is not entirely a structural issue. Please add it to the agenda for tomorrow's morning meeting. I'll see you later. I have some lab time scheduled with Ed."

Without waiting for a reply, she turned and walked out, down the small passageway that lead to a makeshift lab where she had been working through some different issues with regard to the control of multiple gravitational field generators. If she were not under so much pressure she would have truly loved the challenge of this technology. It behaved according to its own set of laws. She had two chief concerns at this point, which was the real reason she had been so upset with Miles. His function was much more independent than hers and Kang's. The two of them interfaced constantly. Miles was now splitting his time between the 5 designers using CAD and the shop floor, dealing directly with assembly issues. Her first major issue was to create a predictive mathematical model so that they could control not merely lifting the massive vessel but steering it in real time. That was where Kang was such a huge help, having his team actively building the control software in such a way that it doubled as their proving ground.

Her second challenge was even more daunting. They started out with absolutely no idea as to how these changing and interacting fields might affect whatever was contained inside the vessel, including people. What if they started this thing up and it crushed everyone on board? What if opposing gravitational fields yanked out all the wiring or interfered with instrument readings? There were a million questions and no time.

Ed continued to be a Godsend, despite the fact that that they seemed complete opposites personality wise at first. After her conversation with Arthur, she had been able to put away the baggage that had plagued their working relationship early on, at least on her end. The result was a new found reliance on him that she would never had thought possible a few weeks ago. He had an uncanny intuition as to the behavior of these systems. Of course it in good part it was from having worked with them so extensively during development, but there was something more. He had an astounding sense of all things mechanical and they had evolved a profound mutual respect for each other's abilities. In addition he seemed to have a unique ability to translate even the most complex and arcane concepts into concrete terms. It was Ed's explanation, not Arthur's that helped her see how to utilize opposing concentric fields to shield and protect the internal structure and inhabitants of the vessel. Arthur understood the theory but Ed had actually done it. Since Ed had completed the fabrication of the last of the gravity generators he had been spending virtually all his time here. Following Arthur's advice, the two of them had a chessboard set up in a corner where they would periodically look to see if a change had taken place. Susan had stopped for a minute while she was waiting to review the board and see if Ed had responded to her last move.

"You're not changing them around while I'm not looking are you."

Susan turned and saw Ed standing there smiling.

"I don't have to cheat to beat you."

Still grinning Ed asked, "No, who do you have to cheat in order to win?"

24

Audrey waited until three days had passed; making certain that she had several public meeting with her attorney. During the course of that time she had carefully played her part by appearing increasingly nervous and agitated.

Hardesty had helped out by having someone identified as one of the companies lawyers leave few ominous messages on her answering machine, nothing directly threatening of course but advising as to the folly of crossing Julius Wingate with such outrageous allegations. It was just the right touch of strong arm tactics to help paint a complete picture for the handlers she was certain were watching and listening in.

During the course of the preceding three days she had repeatedly taken out the business card left by Jack Felman and looked at it nervously, always putting it back.

This time she dialed the number. A familiar voice answered, "Felman."

"Yes, Mr. Felman – this is Doreen Adler. You asked me to call if I remembered anything that might help you."

"Yes Ms. Adler, thank you for calling me back."

"I'd rather not do this over the phone. Can you meet me at my attorney's office? I don't want to be seen going into your office or have you seen coming here. I figure that would be safe."

"I could do that. Will your attorney be present?"

"Should she be?"

Felman sighed, "Ms. Adler, in the first place your attorney practices civil, not criminal law and you are not the target of any investigation, your ex-boss is. You are helping us. If you want your attorney, that is entirely up to you but it has been my experience that under such circumstances, they simply complicate matters under the guise of protecting you. On the subject of protection, I don't wish to frighten you but there are a number of dangerous characters mixed up in this. Your life could be in jeopardy if they felt you were a risk and I doubt your lawyer, no matter how good they are would be interested in stopping a bullet for you."

Audrey almost broke down on the phone, "Oh my God, I was afraid of something like this. Look, just meet me at the Starbucks on the corner in 30 minutes – can you do that?"

"I'll be there."

Audrey hung up the phone and paced rapidly back and forth for effect, then grabbed her jacket, cap and sunglasses then headed out the door. It seemed like they were falling for the act hook, line and sinker.

She made two circles around the block then ducked into the coffee shop, ordered and took a booth near the back of the store. A few minutes later Jack slid into the seat across from her, coffee in hand. He was casually dressed in a white shirt, windbreaker and khakis. He could easily been some office drone who stopped for his mid-day caffeine fix. She knew better.

"Thank you for coming so quickly."

"That's alright. It's a scary business Doreen…may I call you Doreen?"

"Please. It's scary alright. Did you mean what you said about my being in danger?"

"Unfortunately, yes I did. I realize that it is a major imposition but you may want to allow us to put you in protective custody."

"No, no – I don't want to do that. Can't you just watch my apartment or something? I just want to limit our contact as much as possible until this whole thing blows over. There's this one guy in particular that works for Julius. You don't know him. He'd find me."

"That's where you are wrong Doreen. I do know him, which is the reason why I am your first best option. We'll keep an eye on you, discretely. Don't worry a thing. Now you mentioned on the phone that you recalled something that might be useful in our investigation."

"I've been racking my brain over this and it could be nothing but about 6 months ago there was some curious activity, a couple of calls, notes, hurried secretive meetings – just out of the ordinary. I never really knew what was happening because Julius set everything up himself instead of asking me to do it. I remember it because it fouled up some things I already had on his calendar. When I asked him about it he got very funny, angry. It wasn't like him."

Felman was listening intently, "Do you have any idea what was behind it all?"

"Not really but I think it had something to do satellites or the military. In some of the divisions we do a little government and aerospace subcontracting. So that wasn't so out of the ordinary but there was just something in the way they went about it that seemed wrong."

"Is there anything else you remember?"

"There was a man who actually visited the office, twice but it was very late as I was leaving for the day. I asked Julius if he wanted me to stay but he said no, in fact he insisted I go home."

Felman leaned forward slightly, "What did this fellow look like?"

"I'm sorry I never got a good look at him but there was something…he had a funny accent. I think he might have been Russian or Romanian…definitely eastern European."

"Excellent, that's excellent Doreen. That's a huge help, more than you know. Is there anyone else that you can think of in the company that might be able to help us?"

Audrey hesitated, "Look I don't want to get anyone else in trouble."

Felman looked at her sternly, "You can't get anyone else in trouble. Only they can get themselves in trouble. You need to be concerned with Doreen Adler and let other people clean up their own messes. Remember my goal here is to protect you in this process. I can't do that if you aren't completely open and honest with me. If you are worried about someone else, I am going to assume that they are probably a good person just like you that got sucked in over their head. You are not getting them in trouble; you may in fact be helping to get them to get out of trouble."

"Look, I'm sorry. I just don't know...I hadn't counted on any of this. Let me think about it... I'll call you."

She hurried out as Jack watched.

25

Hardesty's small chartered speed boat pulled up alongside of the yacht. He knew the crew had had him under surveillance long before he could actually see them. The vessels height and long range radar capability had surely picked him up as soon as he broke over their horizon. One of the ships officers was there to greet him and direct him into the salon on the observation deck where his host greeted him warmly.

"Ah Hardesty, so nice of you to drop in."

His manners and English were impeccable but then he would never have expected otherwise. His host was fluent in at least 5 languages that he knew of, although any information concerning the gentleman was sketchy at best. Still this was his world and Hardesty knew he had the option of playing by house rules or he would be entertaining the fish. He also knew that if he didn't have a specific appointment and just dropped in as his host suggested there would be no option.

"It was very kind of you to make time for me."

"Not at all, I saw that you had wired my consulting fee right on time as agreed and I must say that the gift you left for my men to pick up was a delightful gesture, a very spirited young lady, but she is coming around."

"Yes, she always impressed me as being adaptive and I must say your home is lovely."

"You are too kind but I am fond of it. Rather fitting I should live at sea since I consider myself a citizen of the world. There are much larger vessels to be sure but then I really don't entertain much. My needs are... simple. Still I can't think of any ships that are better appointed either in their creature comforts or... shall we say in their technological capabilities."

Hardesty smiled politely and replied, "Oh I have had the opportunity to be a guest on a great number of very elaborate private vessels in the course of my work and I would have to say that this ideally suits you."

His host repaid the enigmatic smile with one of his own, "Oh, but where are my manners. I've had the staff prepare coffee. We just departed Port Louis in Grenada and they have the most marvelous locally grown organic cocoa there, the galley laid in a supply and the pastry chef has been outdoing himself as a result. I hope you'll join me."

"Of course, you are too kind."

The two men chatted for 15 minutes over coffee while overlooking the blue waters of the Caribbean but Hardesty had no illusions. This was an interview, pure and simple. Every carefully worded question was designed to probe and test Hardesty's authenticity. This man dealt in wholesale death. He possessed no politics, no inconvenient loyalties. He would and often did sell to mortal enemies and why not – it was good for business. For all their bluster and rhetoric, clients never dared balk at his tactics for fear of being cut off from their best source of supply because that would mean certain death. Once satisfied, the conversation turned to the business at hand.

"So it is my understanding that you are interested in some very unusual and difficult to obtain materials."

Hardesty nodded, "That is what prompted my need to chat with you directly rather than work through one of your distributors, as I normally would."

"You'll find we can speak freely here, this vessel is proof against any prying eyes or ears…It's the ultimate home office. I understand that you are looking for nuclear capability. I just happen to have six MIRV warheads each with a destructive capability of 150 kilotons. It seems some friends of mine liberated them from the Bulava ballistic missile program. The price is $12 million US each, delivered. How many did you want?"

"All of them."

"Wonderful, that should be a hell of a party. Anything else?"

"No actually, I have everything else covered I think."

"Excellent then, you can process payment via the same means you used for my consulting fee. Once we are in receipt, shipment of the merchandise will be consolidated in a consignment of Italian granite. Delivery will take approximately 4 weeks after payment. The granite contains minute traces of uranium to help mask the shielded contents in the event of a zealous inspector with a Geiger counter and nothing better to do but I shouldn't worry, we have friends in various ports of entry."

Hardesty answered, "I have every confidence you do."

The two men rose and began moving toward the door that led to the open air and ultimately Hardesty's waiting craft.

"Do be careful on your way back. There have been sightings of pirates in these waters from time to time. Should you run into any, just tell them you have been to see me and they won't trouble you."

"I would imagine that they are customers, certainly at least they deal with some of your distributors."

"I suppose they do but in any event, they know me. You see a few years ago, shortly after I bought this vessel a few of their brethren attempted to waylay us with the prerequisite AK-47s and a few RPGs. I made it a point to send them back to their leader… not all of them mind you… just some of the best parts along with a note instructing them that they could keep the Tupperware. I haven't had a problem since."

"That's a nice touch. I'll have to remember it."

"Please do. I've enjoyed meeting you Mr. Hardesty but we will not meet again. Good-bye."

26

They were in the last month of their countdown and the massive, silvery vessel, surrounded by catwalks, scaffolds and cranes looked like a gigantic anthill of activity.

Oddly enough, the actual amount of space required within the massive sphere for equipment and crew was relatively small by comparison. The ship only required a crew of four but they had already installed accommodations for sixty eight personnel including showers, lavatory facilities, galley, even a laundry. The people working on the interior of the vessel were actually living on board now and in fact, they had purposely been segregated from those completing work on the exterior for security purposes. In the interest of speed everything that required automated control was being brought in as pre-wired modules. Everything that did not specifically require automation was left as a manual function. In expectation of expanding future applications for the vessel it had been segmented into compartments ready to adapt to changing roles. There were crew quarters, store rooms, space for laboratories, a machinery repair shop… virtually any contingency. Most of the areas were simply empty rooms pre-wired for data and power, waiting.

At the heart of all of this sat the main control and engineering spaces. Here were the computers that controlled and manipulated the gravitational fields for lift and navigation. The electrical generators, life support functions such as air and water purification, ventilation, climate control, communications… everything was housed here. Hundreds of gravity motors had been mounted in a precise geometrical pattern on the interior of the hull and workers were busy pulling cable and systematically connecting them back to main control. With the generators already in place and functioning (the vessel was already self sufficient in terms of its electrical needs) they might be ready to begin 1% power trials in another 8 days at this rate.

At this point Susan, Ed, Miles and Kang were spending every waking moment putting out fires it seemed.

Arthur on the other hand, who had been the catalyst for everything happening here found himself with less and less to do oddly enough. Certainly he was always available to answer questions, help resolve problems and assist in any way he could but the actual construction was completely outside his realm. So he contented himself with puttering in the lab. The difference was that now he had every resource he might conceivably need at his fingertips.

Still he could not help but allow his mind to wander backward at times. If only his Lydia was here, it would be perfect. She had always believed in him. When the laughter of his detractors was still ringing in his ears, she would be there telling him that he would prove them all wrong. Despite the years her absence was almost visceral in the way it still tugged at him.

Work was his only refuge, but the problem was solved and instead of feeling complete he found exactly the opposite to be true. Without his life's mission, without her, it all seemed shallow…empty in a way he could not explain. Of course everyone, even Ed was too busy to listen. So he did the only logical thing he could and he threw himself into unlocking the secrets of his discovery and fortunately every new answer seemed to bring another thousand questions. It filled him again and gave him purpose. Occasionally he would come across some interesting anomaly that had a direct bearing on the project which would cause a flurry of excitement but that would quickly revert to the business at hand and completing the project.

The others would depart, consumed with their own difficulties once again leaving Arthur to the tiny lab that had become his world. For the most part, while academically interesting the overwhelming majority of Arthur's investigations at this point did not have any direct effect on the ship's completion and as a result, while he might get a polite "That's very interesting…" now and then it was fairly obvious that the inventor of the most powerful energy source since the discovery of fire had become incidental to the process.

While his days were occupied, the nights were becoming increasingly difficult. He often found himself just sitting on the far side of building three away from the glow of the construction staring up at the stars wondering who or what might be staring back.

People call them the heavens but he could not help wondering if indeed that was what awaited the results of all these efforts. If there was a heaven it was not out there. It was within him because that was where his Lydia was, his own private angel, watching over him all these years. She remained forever whispering in his ears that it would be alright, that he would prove them wrong some day.

"You were the one who was right. Soon you and I and Ed will show them all," Arthur mused quietly to himself time and again watching the stars dance overhead. Often he would nod off dozing for a time only to wake up hours later still sitting cold, cramped and stiff. But the dream of her was worth it somehow. He would get up and wander back to the lab regardless of the hour. Time seemed to have lost much of its meaning here and the little bed that sat empty in the cubicle that had been his here was just a place to lie awake and restless.

It was on just such an evening that he made his discovery.

He went back over his numbers several times to make certain. There didn't appear to be any mistake. He began by setting up a small scale experiment to confirm his suspicions. He had to be absolutely certain. There must not be any room for error and he could not tell the others. Not even Ed; he could never know. If this was right, it changed everything.

The next day he was able to conduct a very small scale reaction to test the theory and after carefully measuring the results, he reset everything and confirmed his findings.

It was just as he thought. Now the problem was how to proceed? He carefully erased the whiteboard and his related computer files. Then he shredded all his related notes.

He thought about what to do next and decided his best course was to go once more to sit under the stars and talk it over with Lydia.

27

Felman sat on the park bench waiting.

Doreen Adler (at least the woman he thought was Doreen) had finally supplied him with a name, a young engineer, Frank Szweic. According to her they had dated twice but she broke if off because he was about as exciting as long division. However, she also knew that he was involved in some capacity with the top secret project she had told him about.

Once he had a name, it wasn't too hard to track him down and apply the right leverage. He was due here any minute. Now maybe he could finally shed some light on the technology Hardesty had alluded to. Emotion was baggage that someone in Jack's position could ill afford but there was no getting past his long time adversary without it gnawing at him. As far as he was concerned dealing with Hardesty was no different than a rabid dog. This was personal and if he ever had any thoughts of dealing with it unemotionally he was kidding himself.

"Hello Frank."

An angry young man stood directly in front of him glowering, "Who the hell are you?"

Jack looked up and smiled, "I'm the guy who can ruin your life, or give it back to you. Now sit down, shut up, wipe that look off your face and listen."

Frank stiffened visibly but obeyed slumping down on the bench next to the older man.

Jack never looked at the young engineer sitting next to him. He just stared straight ahead and spoke in a low monotone, "Let me lay this out for you. As far as we have been able to determine approximately six months ago your boss and his chief henchman, a fellow named Hardesty conspired with certain foreign nationals to develop an anti-satellite weapon based on some old soviet technology. Stop me if you've heard this one."

"I don't know what you're talking about."

"Really, that's odd because I have it on good authority that you have been right in the thick of it."

"That's a lie, who told you that?

"Oh that's not really important. What is interesting though is that $120,000 you have in a safety deposit box."

Frank swiveled around looked at the older man in complete surprise, "What $120,000? I don't have any safe deposit box. What the hell are you talking about?"

"Oh that's right I forgot. You have a safe deposit box in your name with $120,000 in it. Now in addition to a whole host of different government agencies who would be very curious as to the origin of these funds, I am relatively certain that your employer would be even more interested to learn about your little nest egg. I'll bet they'd be just dying to know where it came from and if I know Hardesty, by the time he was done with you - you'd be dying to tell him."

"I don't know anything about this I told you…wait a minute. You must have planted the money."

"Oh come on, you can do better than that. The cash is in a safety deposit box taken out in your name. It's in an envelope that has your fingerprints on it."

"That's impossible."

"What's impossible? That you handled a large manila envelope and that envelope later turned up with a large quantity of cash in it in a safety deposit box in your name. What are people going to believe? That you are the victim of an elaborate frame up or that you were selling out corporate secrets. Do the math."

Frank looked utterly exasperated, "What do you want from me?

Jack never broke from his soft monotone, "That's better. I just want to help you. Your employer is involved in developing some very dangerous technology and we need to keep tabs on it. It's a question of national security. Now if you help me in addition to being a good citizen and staying righteous with the authorities, I'll give you the location of your safety deposit box."

"Alright, alright…what do you want to know?"

"We'll start simply. What is the basis of the technology, how does it work?"

Frank took a deep breath, "The best way to describe it is that it a force gun. It doesn't fire a projectile. It fires short burst particle beams of highly ionized radiation. Normally ionized radiation would not be capable of traveling any great distance because it strongly interacts with everything around it. The system works for two reasons. It fires from an orbital platform, in space there is little for it to interact with and rapid pulsation sets up a wave the preserves the intensity and integrity of the beam. It has the ability to completely disrupt the operations of a satellite without necessarily damaging it physically. The goal is to not merely destroy an enemy's satellites, but to re-write them, convert them to our use."

"Thank you Frank. That wasn't so hard was it? Don't worry, it will get easier."

"What do you mean?

"I mean I will need a weekly progress report on the project."

Frank buried his head in his hands, "I can't do that. If they find out…"

Jack stopped him, "Then I would strongly suggest that you don't let them find out. Just act normally. Go about your daily routine. Do what you always do. Don't deviate. I have noticed that every Friday you stop off and have a beer at Chester's. Just go right on doing that. I'll arrange to have one of our operatives there for you to hand off the information to. Relax; we're going to take care of you."

"Yeah, that's what I'm afraid of."

28

Hardesty slipped silently into Wingate's office, not that he had to but it was second nature. Julius was used to it by this time of course and while he could never actually get used to it at least it had devolved to the status of mildly irritating.

"Hello Hardesty. Fill me in."

"Good morning Mr. Wingate. The ship is two days from initialing low power trials. The nukes have landed and my people are in the process of recovering and transporting them to a staging area near the site.

"I thought that you wanted to employ a nerve agent as well."

"I reconsidered that. I have made arrangements to divert phosgene gas from one of our chemical facilities. Easy to make, readily available, almost odorless, I've had a sufficient quantity stockpiled at the build site to guarantee us a 100% kill of the construction crews. The nice part is that it can be neutralized with sodium bicarbonate so there is a lot less clean up to contend with, it even occurs naturally in minute quantities. I am also staging more in the vicinity of selected military sites just to increase the general panic."

"Sounds like a good choice."

"Thank you. We've used two of my operatives to position the story that you are developing an anti-satellite "Star Wars" technology in secret. We are calling it a Force Gun; it serves the dual purpose of diverting the attention of certain prying agencies and explains how you just happen to have an alien killing ray gun lying about."

"Nice touch Hardesty, you are always thinking."

"Mr. Treavor has your Escape Tubes installed and I have a handpicked crew of twelve in training. Everything is coming together right on schedule. In fact at this juncture I really only have one source of concern."

Wingate's mood instantly changed, "What concern?"

"We still don't have a lock on the technology. There are a number of huge gaps that are only known to Mr. Phoebus and Mr. Fisher. We've had our crews go over every square in of their house and workshop while they have been on site but they cannot make heads or tails of anything. Whether by mistake or intent, we could have our best and brightest scour that site for the next fifty years and there is no guarantee they could replicate what they created."

"Damn it. I was afraid of that. Isn't there any other leverage we can bring to bear? There has to be a way, what's our Plan B?"

Hardesty shook his head, "We really don't have one. Certainly there are some more primitive means of persuasion but I have my doubts that they would work at their ages. It would probably kill them before we could get what we needed... Although there might be a way but it's rather dangerous."

"What's that?"

Hardesty continued. "Use the throws of addition and withdrawal. If we were to hold them in a secure medical or psychiatric facility and get them addicted to a drug such as morphine, the pain and fear of physical withdrawal could do the trick. The greatest concern would be that they might suffer brain damage in the process, delusions, memory loss."

Wingate sat thinking, "Do we know if there has been any research been done on that, the effect of different addictions and the mental capacities of the elderly?"

"I don't know of any that fit our criteria. I'm fairly sure that have been many studies done on lifelong addition but this would be a case where the length of the addiction would actually be very short. I will put a couple of interns in HR on it. It may be that we'll have to commission a study."

Wingate pursed his lips, "Well we can only hope that it will never come to that, that they can see reason. A study like that would take forever and we could never be 100% certain of the outcome."

"Well fortunately we have a little time before launch. We'll give it some more thought and hopefully they will yet come around."

"Is there anything else?

"No, we have made it a point to stock out the ship with food stores, medical supplies and the like. We want to make certain that to all outward appearances it is design for long term, peaceful missions."

"Wonderful. Let me know when power trials begin. I'll be interested to see that."

29

"Arthur, c'mon it's time" Ed called to his brother in law.

"Oh that's alright; I was trying to finish up something I was working on here. You go ahead with the others."

"What! Forget about it. That'll keep. We're about to initiate a 1% power trial for the first time with the full matrix of the ship. You can't miss that, it's what we've been waiting and working for. C'mon hurry up."

Arthur sighed and a little reluctantly but obediently he followed Ed through a corridor to a bunker that overlooked the sphere. Everything that could be pulled back, had been pulled back and the huge metallic orb sat there partially bathed in the glow from four of the portable towers that had helped illuminate it during its round the clock construction. Kang had remained on board with six of the construction team and spoke to them over a video hookup from his seat at the main control consol that was the heart and soul of the great vessel, "Kang here, all systems read green for go. Ready for initial matrix low power test on your command."

Susan leaned over the microphone, "Gosh Kang, that sounded very official. Just be safe. Stay to the protocol. A thirty second ramp up to 1% power across the full drive matrix, hold for ten seconds and power down. Remember your name is Kang, not Kirk, so don't go flying off."

"Aye-Aye, boss, waiting your command to initiate sequence."

Susan and the rest of the room simultaneously took a deep breath, then she said, "Initiate power trial sequence on my mark...three...two...one...mark."

Every monitor and dial in the room sprang to life.

As soon as Kang hit the key to initiate the preprogrammed sequence it seemed as though the ship came to life. It was as though the surge of energy that pulsed through her hull converted her from inanimate to animate, she was a living thing. Over the next thirty seconds everyone held their breath while the field grew and stabilized at 1% for ten seconds, then it automatically powered down. From the bunker, everyone watched in the pre-dawn gloom as the faintest of blue glows softly shimmered across the surface of the 120 ft diameter sphere and then vanished as though the great ship was falling back asleep.

No one spoke for what seemed an eternity. Then Kang's voice sprang from the speaker, "Everything is rock solid, all readings are well with performance specifications, request permission to go to 5%. Come on, Boss. Let's see what this baby can do."

Susan shot a glance to the others in the room, bit her lip and replied, "Go 5%."

Again the readings jumped. The preprogrammed sequence employed a longer ramp up but this time reached 5% power and held for ten seconds before shutting down.

Susan leaned over the microphone again, "Phenomenal job everybody. Kang, shut her down, you and the others onboard report to the clinic for a complete physical. We will regroup for a team meeting at 11 to compare notes."

"Susan" Kang called out over the speaker. "We have one more important piece of business."

Susan passed a puzzled look around the room, "What, is there a problem?"

"Not a problem, just an important bit of housekeeping. Call me crazy but I got to be here in the very heart of the ship as she came to life. Maybe I am superstitious but she needs a name."

"Well if that is our biggest concern after the initial trial, we're really doing alright."

"I know that it sounds odd but a great ship needs a great name."

Miles broke in, "Oh come now Kang, what's next? Do you want to paint a smiley face on it too, or maybe a cartoon pinup girl? Let the boys in marketing figure that one out, we've got things to do, including you."

Ed stopped him, "No, Kang has a good point. Why the hell should a bunch of clowns that think up soap jingles and car ads get to decide what to name her. After all she's our baby, all 80,000 tons of her. It's only right that we should decide."

Susan turned and put her hand on Arthur's arm, "What do you think Arthur. None of this would exist if it weren't for you. What would you like to call her?"

"Oh well I suppose if it were entirely my doing I would call her Lydia but that hardly seems fitting for such an endeavor. Still I guess that Ed is right, it shouldn't be left to people that name breakfast cereal... hmmm... how about khalix?"

Susan said, "That's certainly interesting, what does it mean?

"It is the Greek word for pebble. Despite all her mass, just like the Earth and the rest of the celestial bodies, ultimately she will be just another pebble in the sky cast about and controlled by the sling of gravity... I don't know, it seems to fit somehow. At least it does to me."

The small group just looked about at each other for a moment until Kang once more broke the silence. "I like it. It is simple, elemental...It makes sense."

Susan looked around once more and said, "Well if there are no objections, I think we have a winner. Gentlemen, I give you the good ship, Khalix."

30

By the time Wingate arrived with Hardesty that afternoon, the onsite medical staff had cleared Kang and his fellow initial crew members with flying colors. Not that they had expected any difficulty. Over the past two months they had logged countless hours in close proximity to fields generated by the devices without any ill effects. This coupled with some specific animal testing they had conducted over that same period as well as the information gathered by Arthur and Ed during development had the team very confident as to the crew's safety from any side effects to exposure.

In fact when Julius walked in, testing had already expanded to include an extended check of the navigational control system. Since he arrived in mid afternoon, the telltale glow was not pronounced in full sunlight. With the vessel powered up all workers were under ground and much of the external support scaffolding and other material had been cleared away. The entire site which had been alive with activity only 24 hours earlier looked deserted.

Wingate burst into the bunker. "Why has work stopped? What's happening?"

Susan turned around and smiled warmly, "Everything's happening."

From the computer monitor Kang and Treavor called out, "Hello Mr. Wingate"

"What do you mean, everything's happening? It was my understanding that you would be starting power trials today."

Still smiling Susan said, "You are seeing them. The Khalix is currently functioning at 28% power as we speak. Miles, Kang and a team of six technicians are currently cycling field polarities to test out ability to navigate."

Wingate looked confused, "If it's ON, why isn't it flying?"

Instead of answering him directly, Susan deferred to Ed who was standing next to her, "Would you mind explaining it, I need to keep an eye on what's going on with the test protocol."

"Not a problem, I got it Sue. Well you see Julius, we know we can attenuate gravity, the trick is controlling it. Remember the generator? It used reversing gravitational polarity to generate electricity, but it didn't float off the table while it was doing it. The technology does not just make matter repel instead of attract, it controls the relative attraction or repulsion of matter using gravity. We can align the gravitational poles so that the ship repels the Earth and rises or we could reverse that polarity and make the ship bury itself into the ground by increasing its attraction for Mother Earth." Ed turned and said to Susan, "How was that?"

Without looking away from the control board Susan replied, "Couldn't have said it better myself."

Ed returned his attention to Wingate, "We have been in power trials since early this morning. Right now we are holding at 28% and have been stable at that level for over half an hour. The Khalix isn't lifting off because that is the way the fields are balanced. Miles and Kang are putting the ship through its paces by repositioning the field balance, right, left, forward, back, up down, just by minor increments to see how rapidly it can react and it is amazing." Ed pointed at the monitor, "Those two did a hell of a job, in flight believe it or not you'll be able to turn this thing on a dime."

Susan spoke over her shoulder, "Actually, the biggest concern in terrestrial flight would be the shock wave. That's the one thing we'll really have to be careful about."

Wingate looked confused, "We never talked about a shock wave, you mean like a sonic boom?"

"Not exactly," Ed continued, "You see the ship moves by attracting matter that lies in the direction it wants to go and repelling matter in the opposite direction. Matter trapped within the field is converted to the field's polarity. Matter that is outside the field is the anchor we push or pull on. The potential problem area is the fringe of the field. That region is exposed to the wall of the field but it is not yet protected by it. Our concern is that if the ship is too close to the ground, moving at a high rate of speed it could crush or tear up everything around it."

Wingate and Hardesty exchanged a quick, knowing glance, "Now you're telling me, that's a hell of a thing to overlook."

Susan broke in, "We are learning this as we go. As long as we are flying at altitudes above 1000 feet, any ground level effect should be minimal. Of course, we need to stay clear of any aircraft or they'd be knocked out of the air."

Wingate shot another glance at Hardesty, "I can see we'll have to be very careful. On a brighter note, you seem very pleased with the testing. On our original time frame we are four days out. What is your prediction will you be able to complete on time?"

Susan again turned to fact Wingate, "Absolutely. The testing is vindicating everything we've done. The check list of corrections is shorter than we had originally hoped. Kang has his people correcting and debugging some of the programming in real time. In fact everything should be ready for launch a day early."

Wingate flashed a smile, "Perfect, I can't wait to see this thing actually fly."

With that the entire team broke out in laughter.

"What's so funny?"

Susan finally managed to catch her breath, "Take a close look at monitor three." Her fingers played across a keyboard and a camera zoomed in on the exterior of the ship.

As Wingate stared he realized that the massive vessel was floating a few feet off the ground, but something was wrong, "Its flying but the picture is all blurry."

Susan said, "Technically, it is hovering and the picture isn't blurry. The ship is rotating at 3000 rpm. It's part of the navigational control test."

Wingate looked back to Ed who said, "I told you it could turn on a dime."

Then he looked back at the main monitor where Treavor and Kang sat calmly at the main control console on board, smiling and waving.

"Unbelievable... Okay that leaves me with two questions, where's Arthur and what's a khalix?"

Ed replied, "Arthur's in the lab working on some pet project. He was here for the first test and it's not a khalix, it's The Khalix —we named her."

31

Wingate and Hardesty sealed themselves into one of the SCIF conference rooms for a few minutes of privacy.

Wingate began, "This thing is incredibly more powerful than I ever dreamed of. I don't want it destroyed. We just need to eliminate the crew and disable it. Then our team of specialists will recover the alien ship. That's the story. That will enable us to keep a lid on everything."

"You are forgetting that everything on board is in English, There are nameplates, trademarks, manufacturer's part numbers on every wing nut on board that thing. The first time anyone enters that vessel they will know it didn't come from anywhere but Earth and people will know the truth."

Wingate thought a moment, "Wait a minute, your cover story, the one you fed to the authorities was that our new force gun would enable us to disrupt the operations of satellites without actually destroying them so that we could turn them to our purposes. Why can't we spin a similar yarn here? Instead destroying the ship our technology permitted us to capture it. Our gun destroyed their computers but we were able to replace their control systems with our own. There is certainly nothing on the gravity things that Ed made in his shop to indicate they didn't come from some other galaxy. Besides by the time that even might become an issue, we're in control. Nobody will question it."

Hardesty thought a moment, "I hate last minute changes. They always increase the chance you'll miss something. Deviating now at the eleventh hour I think is a mistake. The plan was simple – blow up the ship. Instantly you have no witnesses, no muss, no fuss and you are the hero. The people we have positioned as crew members were in part selected because they have no ties. No one would miss them if they vanished in a puff of smoke along with the ship out there. However, if we preserve the ship that means that all crew members not under our control have to be eliminated but we have to have someone left to land the thing and open the door for us. Finding and controlling that person at this late date is the problem. Because the crew we selected purposely has no ties, no families it also means that we have little or no leverage to force them to comply with our wishes if they decide to freelance. You see the problem?"

Wingate bit his lip and stared at his chief conspirator for about 10 seconds before speaking, "You are absolutely right of course... but I want that ship so figure it out." With that he got up and started toward the door, "I'm heading back to the office. I need to see you there at 8 AM tomorrow with an answer."

Hardesty just sat there, as emotionless as ever watching him go. After the door closed behind Wingate, he continued to sit there musing silently for several minutes then got up to go find Arthur. Much as he expected the old gentleman was hard at work scribbling some cryptic mathematics on his white board.

"Hello Mr. Phoebus."

"Oh, good afternoon Mr. Hardesty, I'm sorry I was preoccupied and didn't hear you come in. Can I get you something – a cup of coffee perhaps?"

"No thank you, very kind of you to offer but there is something I do need from you, your kind attention for just a few moments. Could you and Mr. Fisher meet me in the small conference room in 15 minutes? I know that you both are very busy but I promise it won't take long and it will be well worth your time."

Shortly thereafter, Arthur and Ed found Hardesty seated serenely at the small round table where work here had begun about 2 months before.

Ed was obviously a little agitated at having to leave Susan alone in the control bunker while testing was ongoing, "Okay Mr. Hardesty, what is so important?"

Hardesty calmly looked up, "The survival of civilization as we know it. Now would you mind closing the door, please?"

Arthur and Ed moved into the room dumbstruck as the door whispered closed behind them.

Hardesty began, "Let me explain. It seems that Mr. Wingate has not been entirely forthcoming with you it seems. His master plan from the beginning was not nearly as altruistic as he pretended. His objective was to use this ship to fake an alien invasion, then blow it up thereby saving the world and in the chaos that would ensue, rise to world power. Naturally the entire construction crew here would be killed… can't have any pesky witnesses lying about… while you, Kang, Dr. Van Dien, et al would be held incommunicado until he could extract whatever information he needs. After that, Oh well no loose ends."

Arthur looked at Ed and back again, "I can't believe it!"

"You had better believe it. If you take a look in the store room that adjoins Mechanical Room 602A near the crew quarters two levels below this one, you'll find enough phosgene gas to kill everyone at this station 4 times over."

Arthur's knees suddenly buckled and he sank into one of the chairs moaning as he buried his face in his hands, "Oh my God, I've handed absolute power to a madman."

Up until now Ed had been standing like a stone staring at Hardesty, "Why are you telling us this now?"

"Because I don't want to die… The fact that I know all this makes me the ultimate loose end. Do you really think that Wingate could or would allow me to continue breathing? My very existence would pose a threat to him."

Ed nodded, "Then what can we do to stop him?"

"We…" Hardesty laughed completely out of character, "There is no we. I am going to do what I do best, vanish. I have some very valuable bargaining chips hidden away and enough money that I can be quite comfortable. Stopping Wingate is entirely up to you, but it is not as difficult as you might think. All you have to do is cripple the ship. If it doesn't fly, he will simply be a businessman that was duped, that took a very bad gamble. All his problems will come home to roost. People in business have a very long memory when it comes to money. You just can't spend a half a billion dollars that stockholders have trusted you with on a secret project like this and have it fail. He will be financially ruined, probably indicted, very likely he'll do some jail time. In short your invention will never hurt anyone and a very bad man will go away for a very long time. But if that ship flies – you will seal all our death warrants and enslave mankind. It shouldn't be a tough decision and now if you'll excuse me, I have a little packing to do. I am supposed to meet with Wingate at eight tomorrow morning in his office and I really think I need to be long gone by then."

Hardesty rose and got as far as the door before he turned, "Oh yes, I should mention that you really can't trust Miles Treavor. Wingate bought him off. Those escape tubes he installed without telling anyone first - were really designed to jettison bombs. So when you go to sabotage the ship, I'd leave him out of the loop. Have a nice day."

With that he disappeared through the door and down the corridor.

32

It was already past three in the morning.

Arthur and Ed had explained to Kang and Susan what Hardesty had relayed to them.

"So the question remains, "Ed continued, "What do we do now? We can't let that maniac have control of the ship. We can't let him kill all of these innocent people."

"It would be a relatively simple matter to corrupt the control software." Kang said, "That would foul up the project for weeks, maybe even months."

"Yes but the ship itself would be intact." Susan countered, "Eventually somebody would debug the code and we'd all be in the same boat."

"Yes," said Kang, "but it would not look like it had been sabotaged. It would just look like it doesn't fly. That might buy us enough time to ruin Wingate financially. If we just start cutting wires or disconnecting switches they will know that someone is doing it and hook them up again."

Susan shook her head, "You make a good point but the only thing they cannot replicate in the ship are Ed's gravity engines still we can't very well start disconnecting hundreds of those and taking them out for the same reason."

Ed was growing more and more frustrated, "Why can't we just blow the damn thing up?"

"The ship is built like a tank," Susan said, "because we made it out of a tank. We don't have any way to generate a blast that could do enough damage to insure that it couldn't be repaired. In order to be truly effective a blast would have to destroy every one of your engines, Ed or we risk the chance they might rebuild. You also have to remember that if we did that, we would never get a second chance. We are surrounded by this private army Wingate calls a security force. I am pretty sure that they would shut us down in a heartbeat if they suspected anyone was trying to damage the project."

"Wait a minute," Ed stopped them, "We don't have to destroy the ship. We just have to keep it out of Wingate's hands. Are you thinking what I'm thinking…"

Susan and Kang stared at each other for a second and then back at Ed.

"Why not?" Ed continued, "Our testing is about 60% complete. We know it can fly."

Susan shook her head, "Yes, but there are still a host of unanswered questions."

Ed responded, "And what better way to figure them out than on a shack down cruise? Here's how I see it. We can't do a good enough job of disabling her to keep the bastard from eventually taking control of it. Once he does that, we're as good as dead. I'd rather take my chances out there. If we can't control it and we go careening out into deep space, Wingate won't get it and we'll at least be in for one hell of a ride. What do you say, are you game?"

Susan had to admit to herself that the mechanic continued to surprise her, "Yes," she said, "I'm game."

Kang too nodded, "Count me in."

"Good, are there any others you know for a fact you can trust that you want to invite? But remember you can't ask anyone that you are not absolutely certain will say yes to all the conditions. Whether we succeed or crash and burn, we aren't coming back. They have to be good with that."

Susan said, "I know of two of my people that will go."

Kang responded, "And I have three more."

Ed nodded, "Then we are a crew. Let's get the staff here moving as many supplies into the Khalix as possible. We can tell them we want to conduct testing under conditions as close to real world as possible. That sounds plausible enough."

Kang stood up, "I'll speak to the shift foreman about getting people on it."

Ed said, "No I'll do that. You need to make certain that all the data we've accumulated here is erased. I can't think of anyone better than you to handle that."

"And I am going to look into disabling that phosgene delivery system you told me about. Fortunately, the gas is not very stable so it will deteriorate rapidly." Susan said, "By the way, where's Arthur?"

33

The office door opened promptly at eight but to Wingate's surprise it not Hardesty who entered but Arthur.

"Good morning Arthur. I didn't expect to see you. Why aren't you out at the project site?"

"Yes, sorry to barge in on you Julius but I have made a rather remarkable discovery and as it relates to the technology and I knew that you would want to see this as soon as possible." the older man said.

"Well, I'm expecting someone that's the only thing."

Arthur smiled thinly, "Oh I can assure you it won't take long."

"Certainly, let's see what you've got."

"Well, permit me to explain briefly first. If you recall I first got the idea as to functioning of gravitational polarity while musing about the Big Bang theory. I had surmised that it was only a change in the attractive value of gravity could have caused the collapse of all matter in the universe, which in turn gave rise to the idea of gravity being polar, etc."

Wingate smiled politely thinking to himself - get to the point...

"Yes I remember you telling all of us about that."

"Well, with the ship construction going smoothly, I found I had more time to go back and do some additional work on the subject. So I began experimenting with the remotest beginnings of our universe in an effort to understand exactly how the theory might apply in actual practice and I made a startling discovery."

"I see, and what was that Arthur?"

"Well, if a seed particle of highly charged, gravitationally aligned matter were released it would immediately initiate an extraordinarily rapid conversion of surrounding matter to convert to this densely collapsed state, resulting in a gross instability and a significant release of energy due to the mass defect created in the collapse."

"Arthur, I have no idea what you just said."

Phoebus glanced down and frowned slightly then looked up and smiled again, "Basically, it is a means by which any matter can be converted into the equivalent of a thermonuclear device. In short, anything or anyone for that matter could go out with their own version of a Big Bang."

With that Arthur held up what looked like a ball point pen in his right hand and clicked the button. The device glowed sharply as he pointed it toward a very confused looking Wingate. Almost instantaneously he seemed to shrink and vanish only to be replaced by a massive explosion that obliterated the western wall of the room along with portions of the ceiling and floor.

Protected by the field the device generated, Arthur shook his head silently surveying the devastation he had always feared might result from his work then turned to go.

34

Hardesty had made certain to bury the six warheads Wingate had so generously paid for in a deserted zinc mine. The detonators had been crated and shipped to a separate storage facility so that only he had the ability to rejoin the two. It was his combination $72 million dollar insurance policy and retirement fund, but then he had earned it.

He quickly packed taking only what he need but then the nature of his life's work had taught him well not to get too attached to anyone or anything. He carried only enough cash to get him to where he needed to be. Excessive amounts triggered questions he neither needed nor wanted. He could access his accounts from anywhere in the world after all. Far more important were several sets of passports and other identification that he would need to cover his trail effectively.

He quickly went about the room one more time, a force of habit, making certain he had wiped down any fingerprints and removed any other trace of his having been there. After one more look, satisfied he opened the door.

To his surprise, Audrey was standing in the hall just outside. She smiled and he heard three pops in quick succession.

Staggering back into the room, he tripped and tumbled backward over a chair landing on the floor, staining the carpet.

She tossed the small Walther automatic and silencer on the bed and surveyed her handiwork, "Don't worry Hardesty. It won't hurt for long. At this rate you should bleed out in about 10 minutes."

He looked up at her and managed to ask, "Why?"

"Why give you 10 minutes, why not just a clean headshot? I just thought we could chat a moment, so you knew it was me. Oh, it's nothing personal, just business. People like you, Jack Felman and I live in a world of cannibals. It was just your turn in the pot."

"Felman…"

"It wasn't him, but then in your situation does it really matter? Good bye Hardesty. When you get to where you're going…"

He forced what almost passed for a chuckle, "I'll save you a seat."

"Now that's what I like about you. You were always a gentleman. Actually though I was going to suggest that you'll have plenty of old friends waiting for you."

She left locking the door behind her.

35

It was just almost noon before they finished moving stores and water onto the ship carefully stowing food, repair parts and other supplies. Just as they were finishing Arthur strolled up carrying a small bag.

Ed looked at him, "Well your timing is perfect. The work is all done. Where the heck were you anyway? I looked everywhere."

"Oh, I was off site. I had a little housekeeping to take care of."

"Well come on then, time's a wasting."

They entered, sealed the hatch and scaled the series of catwalks the lead to main control stopping only to drop off Arthur's bag. The balance of the crew was bustling about running various system checks.

With his characteristic stroll, Arthur wandered over to Kang who sat busying himself with the controls, "So Captain, when do we blast off?"

Kang pointed, "If you look at the view port, you'll notice that we are already at an altitude of 18,000 miles and accelerating. I have laid in a course that will have us in a synchronous orbit on the dark side of the moon in about 2 hours and 17 minutes. I thought that would be the best place to stop since we'll be undetectable from Earth and we can assess our situation before deciding our next move. After inventorying our supplies, we will probably find we need a few things before departing."

Arthur looked at Kang, "Oh I concur, if we can bring on enough material for say a two year journey that may be sufficient to our needs. Given our ability to travel at relativistic speeds centuries will have passed here at home by the time we return. Who knows, maybe by then they'll be ready for us."

Ed walked over to Susan and said, "Well I know what my next move is. Sue, I know you're a good fifteen years younger than I am. I'm just an old mechanic and you've got degrees I can't even pronounce but I figure I've got to ask you to marry me. I waited until we took off to ask because… well, I have a lot less competition out here."

Susan looked at him in utter amazement, "What… why?"

"Well for one thing you're the only woman who ever beat me at chess. So I guess I have to marry you, otherwise you won't let me win."

Arthur laughed, "Ed, are you in for a shock."

"But how can we get married. There's no one to perform the ceremony. You don't even have a ring… do you?" Susan said.

Ed reached in his pocket and produced a small silvery band, "Made it myself in the machine shop. That's Monel cupro-nickel, that baby will never rust and it won't turn your hand green. As far as marrying us, I figure Kang can do the job. He's the Captain. What do you say?"

"But I don't have anything to wear…"

Ed reached out and took her hand, "What are you talking about? You look great in coveralls. Come on. I'm offering you a honeymoon on the moon, what other excuse do you need."

Susan blushed.

36

Reading from the teleprompter, the evening news went like this:

"The area was rocked today by two massive gas line explosions, one in the suburb of Fernwood where a small home and its adjacent garage belonging to a retired school teacher were completely obliterated at about 6 o'clock this morning, then approximately 2 hours later a second blast severely damaged several of the upper floors of the RSS Technologies building downtown. Miraculously in both instances no bodies were found in the wreckage and it is believed that no one suffered injury. Julius Wingate, CEO of RSS could not be reached for comment.

On the lighter side of the news, earlier this evening in the remote town of Grosbeck Falls, it seems that aliens visited an all night market according to the store manager, Silas Peabody who reported the appearance of a massive round spaceship. In case you are curious, he says that E.T must be particularly fond of frozen pizza and beer. It seems that they took all that he had in stock among other things although one of the extraterrestrial visitors made another put back several boxes of cigars. According to Mr. Peabody, they were polite, paid cash and left him a nice tip. He also added that they can come back anytime. I guess if that store manager thing doesn't work out, Mr. Peabody can always get a job in intergalactic relations.

…and that's the news, good night folks."

About the Author

Paul Holland is an inventor, writer, speaker and entrepreneur. He has worked in a number of different fields including biotechnology, nuclear power, environmental, fluidics and the exhibit industry.

He and his wife live in a house he designed and built himself in New Jersey. They consider their three children their greatest accomplishment.

"G" is his first novel.